MW01596758

JEANNE BANNON

invisible

INVISIBLE

Jeanne Bannon

Dedication

This book is dedicated to the women in my life.
In particular my mother, Nina, my grandmother "Mama"
and my daughters, Nina and Sara.

Chapter One

"Lola, get your suit on and help supervise the pool," Justine, the athletic, sun-kissed, twenty-one-year-old camp director orders once we get off the bus. "The more eyes the better."

Immediately my heart takes off in a sprint. "What? Why?" I try to hide the wobble in my voice.

Curious, expectant gazes turn to me as my fellow counsellors wait with evil half-smiles for my reaction. Although I haven't told a soul, except my best friend Charlie, how I feel about wearing a bathing suit, they know my private horror. It's the horror of every fat girl.

Justine flips through the sheets on her clipboard. She runs a finger down the column of names. "No campers will be sitting out today."

The impossible has just happened. Not one kid was sick, or had left their bathing suit at home. In my three summers as a counsellor, not once has this happened.

For a long, awkward moment, I stand frozen in place wondering how to get out of this. A sudden migraine? My period? My mouth opens, but no words come.

Justine leaves and with her, my chance for escape. I'm left teary-eyed, searching through my bag for my black one piece. Stuffing away the panic, I march past the onlookers, who I have never considered my friends despite working with them the entire summer. In the change room, I find an empty stall and with great reluctance, pull on my suit.

It's my last day of work as a camp counsellor at Inglewood Day Camp. My group of kids consists of eight six-year olds — four boys and four girls. On Thursdays we take the campers to the local outdoor swimming pool. It's a short ride, only five minutes on the creaky old school bus and my job is to watch the kids who won't be swimming;

either because they don't feel well, or they've forgotten their swimsuits. Believe me, this job suits me just fine. As a matter of fact, I volunteered for it.

Not only am I fat, I'm freakishly tall. God only knows why, since Mom is petite and Dad is on the short side. My older sister Eva is the spitting image of Mom, fair and fine boned. I take after Dad's side, bulky, dark and thick. Dad says I must have gotten some of Uncle Sammy's genes, the giant of the Savullo family, who tops out at 6ft 4 inches. Anyway, I'm sure you're getting a good mental picture right about now.

My insides drop as if I placed a foot on a step that wasn't there when I peer down at the coarse dark hair creeping from my calves to just past my knees, where it gradually peters out. Then I run a hand across the tops of my thighs. The triple bulge of my belly prevents me from a good look at my sorely neglected bikini area. Even in the blazing August sun, I wear baggy cotton Capri pants, never exposing more than an ankle. There's never been a reason to shave. My eyes mist with tears, but I pinch them away. It'll be hard enough to go out in public like this, but I won't give *them* the satisfaction of seeing me cry. I lift my chin in resolve and open the door.

The whistle blows, signalling the beginning of the session. Screams of delight fill the air, as the kids jump into the pool to find relief from the 90-degree heat.

I fasten a towel around my waist as best I can. Towels never seem large enough to wrap completely and comfortably around the bulge of my stomach. To the pool I go, treading silently so as not to draw attention.

"Where's Lola?" Sonia, a fellow counsellor, asks.

At first I think she's joking because I'm right in front of her. I toss her an annoyed look and don't bother to answer as I trudge past to the edge of the pool, where I pull off my towel and slip into the water.

"She's probably taken off," Jerod replies. He's a year younger than I am, but looks older with his muscular build and chiselled jaw line. The girls love him. "I hope she doesn't show," he continues. "Who wants to see a hippo in a bathing suit anyway?"

Sonia laughs, a little too hard and places a hand on Jerod's shoulder.

Puzzlement and anger compete on my face. I'm standing no more than three feet away from them. I'm used to rude comments and I know what everyone thinks of me, but this is way beyond mean. The tears in my eyes spill down my cheeks and I slip under the water, hoping to wash away the evidence of my pain. Not that anyone would care, but crying could give them more ammunition; just another reason to taunt me.

Kids bounce around me, laughing and playing. Justine stands like a sentinel, looking like a Bay Watch babe in her red suit, one hand gripping an emergency flotation device. Her steel blue eyes are focused on the activity in the pool.

Jerod jumps in, nearly landing on my back. I barely have time to leap out of the way. My anger boils; blood rushes to my temples and pounds there, giving me an instant headache. I hurl myself at him, pushing with all my might, elbows aimed at his chest. I hit nothing but air and fly into the rough concrete wall of the pool, scraping a hole in my one piece and rubbing raw a patch of skin. Small blood pinpricks rise to the surface.

"Hey!" I scream, bewildered. How'd he manoeuver out of the way so fast?

Jerod slips under the water and emerges at the other end of the pool in one long, slick glide.

The steel in me comes up, anger replacing humiliation. I pull my bulk out of the water and march over to Justine.

"Did you see what that asshole just did?" I bellow.

Justine brings the whistle that hangs from her neck to her lips and blows two sharp blasts, making my ears ring.

"Stop horsing around," she calls to a group of boys, who offer sheepish grins and stop instantly.

I step forward so she can see me. "Justine?" I reach to touch her shoulder but, impossibly, my hand falls *through* her.

"Justine?" I call again, louder, my voice panic-laced. With both hands, I grab her, or *try* to. Again, it's as if she's not there.

My mind is swept along in a current of anxiety. *What's happening?*

Then it hits me... it's me who's not there.

Chapter Two

Eight months later . . .

I love Sunday afternoons. That's the day I spend time with Grandma Rose, my maternal grandmother. My sister Eva hasn't bothered much with her since she found a boyfriend, not that she spent much time with Gran before that anyway. But now she has an excuse not to visit her eighty-year-old grandmother. Age doesn't matter to me. Grandma Rose is the coolest person I know and I adore being with her. She's very creative and loves to sketch and paint in watercolors, acrylics and oils. Her apartment is jam-packed with artwork.

After turning my key in the lock, I almost trip over a canvas as I make my way into her small one-bedroom apartment. Last year she gave me a key of my own and told me, "Just come on in anytime, Kiddo." And so I do.

"Hey, there's my girl," Grandma Rose says, a huge smile on her paint-smeared face. Her auburn hair sticks up in all directions, looking as if she hasn't bothered to run a comb through it this morning. She was probably too eager to start painting. Nevertheless, you won't find a white hair on Gran's head. She's diligent with her dye jobs. White hair makes a woman old, she says.

She's standing in the solarium off the living room where the light's best. A canvas almost as tall as she is sits on an easel. Grandma Rose is short and I feel like a beast beside her. I don't think she's even five feet tall.

"Hi Gran," I say as I walk over to take a peek at her latest creation. I'm met with a startlingly huge portrait of John Travolta from his "Welcome Back Kotter" days. I give my head a slow shake of wonder and stifle a giggle.

"What made you paint this?" I ask.

"Oh honey, I just go with whatever pops into my head and this morning it was John."

I don't have the heart to tell her the only way I knew it was John Travolta was by the picture resting on the table beside her paints. Grandma Rose may be bursting with creative juices, but she has little real artistic ability. But as long as she doesn't know it, what does it matter? It's what makes her happy and I'm happy when she's happy.

Gran moves to the kitchen to rinse off her brushes and eyes me suspiciously. "Somethin' the matter?" she asks.

She's a human barometer of emotion. It's like she's psychic, at least when it comes to me. She can tell by one glance whenever something's not quite right.

"The usual," I reply, throwing my bulk onto the overstuffed couch.

"Did it happen again?" she asks.

Grandma Rose isn't talking about the invisible thing. I haven't told her about that. I haven't told anyone. What could I say anyway? No one would believe me. Gran's asking whether my mom has embarrassed me yet again; our usual topic of conversation and my usual complaint.

My vanishing episode happened eight months ago and so far, it hasn't happened again. Thank God, 'cause I really freaked out when no one could see or hear me that day at the pool. It was only for a few minutes, but it felt like a small forever. I'd never been so happy to be the butt of a joke as I was when I heard the laughter and saw the fingers pointing in my direction. That's when I knew I was back, hairy-legged and fat. Everything back to normal.

The events of that day roll around in my mind a lot and I've tried to figure out what happened. I even did a Google search and the only things I came up with were that I had a hallucination, or somehow slipped into another dimension. I'm not sure about either of those explanations and as time passes, the more unreal it seems. Maybe it was just a dream.

Grandma Rose heaves a sigh. Her shoulders rise and fall as she continues to clean paint-speckled bristles. "Your mom's always been kinda different. I don't know what else to tell you. She certainly doesn't take after me."

"Well, she's not like the other moms," I say, toeing off my sneakers.

My mother Heidi is forty-four going on twenty-one. She's my opposite in every way. Where I'm big and awkward like an ox, she's small and dainty. I wear comfortable running shoes and live in T-shirts and baggy sweats and she wears tight designer jeans, four-inch spikes and low-cut tops. Make-up for me consists of a little black eyeliner and pale lip-gloss. Mom is always so done up she looks like a hooker or, at best, a stripper ready for the stage. The gym and the hair salon are her homes away from home. But what I find the most horrifying are her tattoos and piercings.

"I've tried talking to her, but you know how she can get," Grandma says, turning to me. "Did something happen?"

I pick at my chipped black nail polish and wonder if it's really Mom I'm upset with, or is it the fact I don't fit in with my own family? I'm not like them, any of them, not my mom, my dad, or my sister. Gran's the only one I can relate to.

"No, Gran. But something will. It always does."

Grandma Rose grabs the kettle and fills it. "How about a cup of tea? You wanna play Sing Star?" Her eyes brighten with the words.

I nod and smile, knowing how much Grandma Rose loves her Play Station 3 and all those singing games.

"Oh good," she says with a giggle.

She sets the kettle on a burner and claps her hands, and in less than a minute I'm singing to the 90s with my eighty-year-old grandmother.

Chapter Three

I always leave Grandma Rose's apartment with a smile on my face and an ache in my heart. I wish my mother were like her. How lucky for my mom to have such a wonderful, almost normal, mother. I'm stuck with a parent in an ever-present state of adolescence, whose life's mission is to desperately hang onto what's left of her looks. My mom, with her rat's nest of hair stacked high on her head, dyed cherry red with chunky blonde highlights and dark brown lowlights, and extensions thrown in for good measure. *A woman can't ever have too much hair*, she's forever saying. Giving me her version of what passes as parental advice. I prefer Gran's words of wisdom – "extensions make a woman look trampy" and "dye your hair only when the white comes in." It seems more dignified, because I think a woman *can* have too much hair.

Dad's just as bad, with his funky jeans, Ed Hardy T-shirts, pointy-toed boots, pierced ears, tattoos and a soul patch. He's going to be *fifty* next year, for God's sake. The thought makes me cringe. I live with dim-witted middle-aged teenagers.

Gran tells me all the time it's not what's on the outside that's important and I know she's right. I suppose I'm a bit of a hypocrite, since I'm always complaining about my weight or my height, or the fact I don't have a boyfriend. But I'm supposed to be obsessed with fitting in and with my looks; after all, I'm the teenager.

It's only a ten-minute walk home from Gran's. I tilt my face toward the sun, soaking in the warmth of the spring day as I make my way along familiar streets. When I approach the park on the corners of Whiteside Avenue and Moorehouse Drive, I stop dead. Sudden dread causes the beat of blood to fill my ears.

There are three boys and a girl – Nino Campese, Tyler Campbell, his girlfriend Julia and Jon Kingsbury. They're seniors like me and even though we've known each other since kindergarten, once adolescence hit and separated the weak from the strong, the cool from the nerd, I became prey. I was hunted by those better looking, and with more attitude, simply for their entertainment.

I plunge my hands into the pockets of my jean jacket and hang my head. Taking large quick steps, I tread quietly. They're talking and laughing and the foul scent of cigarette smoke wafts past me in the breeze. From the corner of my eye, I spot Julia and Tyler sharing a butt as they cling together under the large plastic orange slide. Nino's holding court and Tyler's laughing at something Nino has said and Jon – well Jon just stands there, looking bored.

Why is *he* with *them*? My heart sinks. I thought Jon was different.

Tyler's eyes flicker my way; immediately I pick up my pace.

"Hey!" someone yells.

I don't answer.

"Where do you think you're goin', ya fat cow?" Nino hollers, as he jogs up beside me followed by Julia and Tyler.

"Home," I say, not stopping.

Nino jumps into my path. "Where's your girlfriend, Savullo?" He sneers and spits a snotty gob at my feet.

"Lesbo freak," Julia chimes in and flicks a butt at my face.

It bounces off my chin with a burning sting. I glare down at her with her hawkish nose and eyes that are too close together. "Get out of my way," I growl through gritted teeth and try to step around them, but Tyler grabs my elbow, his fingers bite into my flesh and a small groan escapes me.

"We're not done talkin' yet, hippo," he snarls.

I yank free. Tears sting my eyes and the heat of anger and embarrassment reddens my face.

"Leave me alone!" I scream and push. Tyler's tall, but skinny and I manage to knock him on his ass. But as soon as I take a step, Nino and Julia are on me.

"Leave her alone," Jon calls. He hung back from the action and is still standing by the orange slide.

I slam a shoulder into Julia's face and hear a crunch as my bulk meets her nose. Blood spurts and the purple blur of manicured nails flash past, as she whips a hand to her face.

She gazes up at me in surprise. "You broke my nose, you bitch!" Then she looks at Tyler with eyes that say "you better do something about this."

My heart beats so hard, the swishing of blood in my ears is a roar. They're swearing, yelling and threatening me, but panic has taken over as adrenaline pushes into my veins, and I make out nothing coherent.

I turn and try to run back the way I'd come. But another hand is on me, biting the flesh of my upper arm through the fabric of my jacket. Then a fist smashes into the back of my head. "You're nothin' but a fat dyke."

My knees smack the gritty concrete as my legs buckle, and deep heaving sobs erupt from me. *Why do they hate me?*

"Where the hell did she go?" Nino asks, his voice laced with astonishment.

"Holy shit!" Julia and Tyler exclaim at the same time. "What the…?"

Slowly, I pivot and look at them. They're turning in circles, searching for me.

Jon is with them now. "She's gone," he whispers in wide-eyed disbelief.

"What? How?" Nino asks.

I creep away on elastic legs.

Chapter Four

I don't stop running until I'm home. I have no idea if I'm still invisible or not until I sprint through the front door and past my sister.

"Slow down," she yells as I fly past her to my room.

I hurl my bulk onto my bed. The old frame groans and creaks in protest. The last thing I want is for Eva or my mother to come running, so I cry into my pillow to silence my sobs. For Eva, my suffering would be entertainment. Mom would hover and try to make me tell her what was wrong. But what was wrong with me was something she could never understand; something she could never relate to. Even now, at forty-four, she's one of *those* people; one of the popular, the cool, the elite.

Do you know how it feels to be the geek in your own family? In high school, she and Dad were the king and queen of the nerd hunters. Ironic, isn't it? I never tell her squat. You'd think by now she would realize I'll never confide in her.

After fifteen minutes of feeling sorry for myself, I shift onto my back and fish my cellphone from my pocket.

Can u come over? I type and hit send.

A second later my best and *only* friend Charlie answers, *give me 5 mins – helping to put away groceries.*

Hurry, I text back.

The book on my night table catches my eye, *The Stand*, by Stephen King. For a moment I contemplate reading until Charlie gets here, but I'm too upset, even though reading and writing are the things I love to do most in the world. Instead, I decide to change and wash my face.

Charlene, aka Charlie, has been my best friend since grade one. She's an only child. Her parents are divorced and her greatest thrill in life is pissing off her mother. Charlie is fair and freckled and a natural blonde, but she dyed her hair black with a shock of bright purple running across the front of her short bob. She's got a nose ring, a pierced eyebrow and a tattoo of a skull on her forearm, which I think is cool. Charlie usually wears her attitude on her face – mean and snarly, but her outsides don't match what's on the inside. I'm the only person close enough to her to actually know Charlie's secret – she's a sensitive girl with a heart of gold.

My parents have tattoos and piercings, but I absolutely hate theirs. They look ridiculous and I'm embarrassed by them. There should be a law that those things aren't allowed once a person hits thirty.

After cleaning myself up, I plop back down on my bed and rub my temples, which are beginning to pound with pain and irritation. I don't know what's more upsetting, the bullying at the park or that I disappeared again. The events of the day run through my mind, and I try to convince myself that in time none of this will matter.

Nino and Tyler will probably end up as janitors and Julia will get knocked up and be a welfare mom. I, on the other hand, have a bright future. I'm going to university to major in English literature and will be a best-selling author, the female Stephen King. I've already had two short stories published and even got paid $20 for one of them. A small smile settles on my lips. Writing, Grandma, and Charlie are my life. I don't know how I would survive if any of them were taken from me.

The thought of Jon Kingsbury hanging with those losers nags me. He's not like them. I've had a crush on Jon since fourth grade. He's tall, a lot taller than me, and I think he's adorable. He's not the most popular kid in school and the girls aren't exactly crazy for him, but he's cute in what Gran would describe as "he'll grow into his looks" kinda way. He's got dark brown, curly hair that rests at the top of his collar, dark blue eyes and wildly deep dimples. He's about 6ft 3 inches but on the skinny side and his nose is a little too big for his face, but when he gets older and puts on some weight, he'll be cuter. I think that's what Gran meant about boys like him growing into their looks.

At school, it's just Charlie and me most of the time, but Jon's always friendly and nice. My stomach lurches at the thought of him being a part of what happened to me today.

The doorbell rings and Eva answers it. A moment later, Charlie's in the doorway of my bedroom, decked out in her usual; an over-sized T-shirt and black skinny jeans with a studded belt.

"So?" she says, settling beside me on the bed.

My room's still decorated as if I were twelve; white furniture and pink walls. I've begged Mom for years for a more age-appropriate room, but pink is *her* favorite color and so pink it will stay. I did, however, manage for my Barbie lamp to meet with an unfortunate "accident," and it was replaced with a cool lava lamp.

"I had a bad day," I say and dab my eyes with a balled up Kleenex.

Charlie grabs my shoulders and holds me at arm's length. "Are you crying?"

I nod.

Although she's sensitive, Charlie's not the overtly emotional type. As a matter of fact, I've never seen her cry; not even when her parents divorced, but she's a good listener and always has great advice.

"Your mother?" she asks.

"No." I don't know where to begin; with the bullying or with the disappearing. I decide on the bullying and get every detail out as fast as I can before the tears really start to flow 'cause then I won't be able to talk.

"Jee-sus. What the hell's the matter with those assholes?" she says and pulls me in for a hug. "Don't worry. They're just a bunch of losers anyway." She smoothes my hair.

I hug her back, thankful to have such a wonderful friend. "There's something else," I say, breaking away and holding her gaze.

She furrows her brow. "Is it bad?"

I shrug, not really knowing how to answer. "You tell me."

She leans back against my headboard, eyes on me, waiting.

"Sometimes I disappear."

Chapter Five

I tell Charlie how I disappeared for the first time at my camp counsellor job and then tell her about what happened today. She sits wide-eyed, jaw hanging nearly to her chest.

"You are shittin' me!" she exclaims.

"No, it really happened. Really, Charlie, you've got to believe me."

She leans closer, squinting, as if examining me to see if I'm telling the truth. "People can't just vanish into thin air," she says finally.

I exhale, disappointed. "You don't believe me?"

"I believe that *you* believe you disappeared."

Tears spring to my eyes and I walk to my desk, sitting with a dejected thud onto my wheeled chair. The chair and I roll a few feet on the hardwood.

Charlie sits up and crosses her legs. "What does everyone else have to say about it?"

I throw her a look of disbelief. "I haven't told anyone else. Who would believe me? I thought you would, but obviously not." I cross my arms tightly over my chest.

"Well, I thought you'd at least tell your grandmother," she replies curtly, but then she runs a hand over her face and her voice softens. "Look, if you say it happened, then who am I to doubt you?" She smiles and throws me a wink.

Relief floods through me and I return her smile.

"Now the question is why and how is it happening?" she says.

I shrug.

"Can you do it now?"

"Doubt it." A frown creases my forehead. "Eight months has passed from the first time it happened to the second. Who knows, it may not ever happen again." My words are more of a wish than a statement. Despite getting me out of a dangerous situation, winking out into Never

Never Land freaked me out. What if I flip into some alternate reality and stay there?

Charlie pauses and taps her pursed lips. The wheels are turning. "Stand up," she says and I do. "Okay, think about what happened to you today. Bring back those feelings of anger and embarrassment. How did it feel when Nino called you a pig? Or was it a hippo?"

Unexpected tears well in my eyes and I feel my cheeks redden with her words. Right now I just want the feelings to go away, not re-live them. I begin to protest but Charlie waves me quiet.

"I think it has something to do with your mental state, either anger or embarrassment or both," she says, pacing around me in a tiny orbit; the wheels still turning.

Maybe Charlie's looking for proof. She doesn't really believe me and won't until she sees it for herself. So, resigned, I close my eyes and sink back into the trauma of the day. The taunts, the vulgar names, echo through my head, as real and hurtful as the moment they were so callously hurled at me, making me want to shrink into a compact ball of nothingness. I feel the blow to the back of my head and my heart jackhammers against my rib cage. I see Jon and that's the worst of it, because I know he sees me too. He's witnessing my nothingness, my worthlessness, my shame.

"Oh my God!" Charlie shouts.

My eyes snap open. "What?"

"You...you...you flickered," she exclaims, a hand over her open mouth.

"I what?"

"It was like you winked out for just a half a second. But holy shit, I believe you! You can make yourself invisible."

A half-hearted smile settles on my lips. I shouldn't have had to prove anything to her. If Charlie was truly my best friend she would have taken me at my word, but I let my hurt feelings slide because an exciting thought occurs to me. Maybe it won't be so bad if I can learn to *control* my newfound "ability." My mind reels at the possibilities.

"You're a freakin' superhero," she says, jumping joyfully into the air.

We spend the rest of the evening talking about the potential of my new power; including the possibility for sweet revenge. Most of our ideas are silly and, invisible or not, I don't think I'd have the guts to pull them off.

"You can walk into the guys' locker room and take pictures of some of the shitheads who make our lives miserable," Charlie suggests. "Especially that asshole Nino. Then we can post them on YouTube."

"Are you kidding? He'd probably love that. He's so conceited." Nino's a star athlete with the body of a Greek God.

"But we could Photoshop them and give him a small dick." She laughs wildly. "He probably already has one, that's why he's so mean." Then her expression changes as a sudden thought hits. "But what if the camera's not invisible?"

"Hmmm, good point." I ponder this for a second. "But my clothes must have been invisible when I vanished or else everyone would have seen them."

"So then if you're holding something when you disappear, it must disappear too," Charlie says, wagging a finger.

A nervous laugh escapes me. "Don't get your hopes up. Invisible or not, I don't have the guts to go into the guys' locker room." Just the thought of it gives me butterflies and makes me want to puke.

"Okay, we'll do some brainstorming and see what else we can come up with." Charlie sits back down on my bed and leans forward. "Where do you think you go when you vanish?"

I throw my hands up. "Don't know."

"Do you see other beings? Like aliens or ghosts?" There's a hint of excitement in her voice.

"No. Everything looks exactly the way it normally does. I can see everyone and everything, they just can't see me."

"I think you're wishing yourself invisible," she says with a thoughtful furrowing of the brow.

"What?" I ask, bewildered.

"Think about it. Think about what was happening to you when you vanished. You were in situations where you literally wanted to disappear, and so you did."

I fall backwards onto the bed beside her and stare up at the spackled ceiling. Something inside me nods in agreement. "You may be right," I say and place Charlie's idea high on my list of possible explanations.

Chapter Six

It's Monday morning and despite the horror of the previous day, I'm in a fairly decent mood as I make my way downstairs to the kitchen. A low rumble of excitement stirs in my belly at the thought of my super power. For the first time in my life, I feel special, plus I've got one whopper of a secret.

Our house is a reflection of my parents' messed-up sense of style. It looks like it's from another time and place; a mix of 70s hippie and 90s new age. The kitchen is mossy green with brown accents as if decorated with bits and pieces of Mother Earth herself.

Wall-to-wall blue shag carpeting covers the floors of the living and dining rooms, and the chrome and glass furniture gives our house just the right hint of crazy. My parents aren't hippies or new-agers; they're just weird.

Eva and Mom are chatting and Dad has left for work already. He's always the first one out the door, needing only his jumbo coffee and a cigarette and he's good to go.

"Morning," I say, filling the kettle and putting it on a burner for my instant oatmeal. Mondays usually start with me on a diet, but by mid-week all good intentions are out the window.

Eva raises a perfectly plucked brow and turns to me. "Why are you in such a good mood?"

She's two years older than me, and is in her final year of beauty school. Mom dropped out of the Revlon School of Cosmetology in her first year. She said it was to start working so she and Dad could get married, but I did the math and I think it was 'cause she was knocked up. Now Eva's living Mom's dream — all the free dye jobs, manicures and facials thrill Mom to no end.

"I don't know," I tell my sister. "It's supposed to be a nice day. Summer's almost here."

"That reminds me," says Mom, her ridiculous multi-colored hair piled high in a wobbly tower of curls. "We've got to go shopping for your graduation dress."

My shoulders deflate, along with my mood. The kettle whistles. I fix my breakfast and sit down at the table. "Can we talk about this later?" I ask, avoiding her gaze.

Mom leans forward, resting her still made-up face in her hands. I suspect she either doesn't remove her make-up at night, or she gets up earlier than everyone else and applies it again. In all my seventeen years, I've never seen her without a made-up face. She peers out from her mass of locks and regards me with steely determination.

"You're not getting away with this one, Lola. You denied me the opportunity to help you get all pretty for the Prom and you're not going to do the same thing with your graduation party." She wags a finger at me.

"I don't even want to go to graduation let alone the party. Pleaaassee Mom, don't do this to me."

"Do this to *you*?" Her voice is shrill. "You're the one robbing *me* of a special moment between a mother and daughter. I'm looking forward to seeing you in a pretty dress, with a little make-up on for a change. And that hair, God, we've got to do something with that hair." She turns to my sister. "What do you think, Hon? An upsweep or something a little wilder?" The way she says "wilder" scares me a little.

I cringe. If only my dim-witted sister hadn't dropped out of high school in her senior year. Then maybe Mom would have been content with her Prom or grad party. I'm certain Eva would have loved all the attention and being made-up like a ten dollar prostitute.

Eva opens her mouth to speak, but I cut her off. "I'll go to grad, but not the party," I say with as much authority as I can muster.

Mom stands, all five foot two of her, and peers down at me. Sitting, I'm still almost her size. Both hands are planted firmly on her hips and, even though I could hip check her into next Thursday with little effort, I hang my head.

"You and I *will* go shopping for that dress and you *will* go to that party, like it or not!" Looking like a child in her bulky terry cloth bathrobe, she stomps from the kitchen.

"I can't understand why she's forcing me to go. What difference does it make to her?" I say with little hope of support from my sister.

"She wants to know you're a girl," Eva says.

I whip my head around to face her, my eyes narrowed. "What the hell does that mean?"

Eva shifts her gaze and suddenly looks sorry for opening her mouth. "You know. She just wants to make sure you … that you like boys," she says quickly, then gets up and leaves.

I'm left alone with my anger. Why does everyone need me to be something that I'm not? Does Jon think I'm some kind of freak? Or that I'm a lesbian and not for him? I'm starting to feel like I want to disappear again when Mom returns dressed in skinny jeans and a sparkly scoop-necked top; spiky heels click on the ceramic tiles.

"Get goin', you'll be late," she says coldly and, to my disappointment, I know I'm still visible.

Chapter Seven

I slam the door to my locker and click the lock in place. Hugging my books to my chest, I start for homeroom.

"Hey, Lola, wait up," a distant voice calls. I squint and spot Charlie. Right now she's not much more than a dot on the horizon as she runs toward me.

"Hi," I answer when she finally arrives and walks with me. Usually she trudges, playing the brooding emo thing to the max, but today there's a bounce in her step and a smile on her lips.

"What's with you?" I ask.

She bounces in front of me and walks backwards. "Oh come on, you know."

A smile plays on my lips as I think about my super power, but it fades quickly because I'm still upset about having to go shopping with my mother.

"Yeah, I guess it's pretty cool," I say.

"Cool's an understatement." Charlie stops and I nearly slam into her. She leans in close and whispers, "I've got an idea."

"For what?"

"You know," she says and gives me a knowing look.

"Oh," I say as realization dawns. "What is it?" I feel obliged to ask, but don't *really* want to know.

"Tell you at lunch." Her smile is bright as she hops off to art, the only class she likes. I wave and continue on to English lit, wondering about her idea. My stomach tenses at the possibilities.

English is the only class I have with Jon. He sits in front of me, which can be a good thing, because I get to stare at the back of his head every day, but it can also be a bad thing, because he's a distraction. Mrs. Wright is rambling on about *Wuthering Heights.* I listen with one ear, but both my eyes are glued on Jon. What's he thinking? How I wish I could read his mind. Or maybe not. What if he thinks I'm a loser like everyone else seems to?

Still, a small part of me wants to reach out and run my hands through his thick curly hair and another part wants to slap him. He's so cute and usually so nice, but I can't get the thought of him with Nino and Tyler out of my head. What does he see in them? Have I pegged him wrong all these years?

I pull my attention away from Jon when Mrs. Wright says she's giving us some class time to begin our essays. I yank my journal from my knapsack and start to write, only I'm not starting my essay, I'm writing my short story. The short story I plan to enter for the Bridgewood High creative writing scholarship award. The winner receives a partial university scholarship. My heart quickens at just the thought of it. There aren't many teenagers jazzed about writing like I am, but for me the contest is a Godsend. It's given me something to look forward to and helps keep my mind off my troubles.

"Hi."

I peer up from my journal to find Jon staring at me. His dark blue eyes seem friendly enough, but I look away dumbfounded, unsure of his intentions.

"Do you have a pen I could borrow?" He holds up a disgusting looking Bic that's been chewed and mangled. "Mine's a good for nothing piece of shit." He flings it over his shoulder and smiles.

A warm flush rises from my collar to my neck and spreads into my cheeks. "Uhh," I say and fumble through my pencil case. My fingers feel fat and rubbery. Finally, they close on a pen. I give it to him and hope he doesn't notice the tremble in my hand.

"Thanks," he says, taking it. He starts to turn around, but hesitates and turns back to face me. He holds my gaze. I want to look away, but I can tell he has something to say.

His lips part and he says quickly, "Sorry… about yesterday."

He turns back to his work before I can reply and my heart does a little jump for joy.

* * * *

I meet Charlie for lunch at our usual table. She's already there and has started in on a pile of gravy-smothered French fries. I take the top off my plastic Tupperware container filled with the remnants of last night's stir-fry. Mom is the reigning queen of stir-fry. I'm so sick of it, I usually buy my lunch when I have the money. Not today, though. This week's allowance was forfeited because I went over on my cellphone minutes. I eye Charlie's lunch enviously.

"My mother's making me go shopping for my grad dress with her," I say, shovelling a forkful of rubbery chicken and soggy noodles into my mouth.

"No way! How're you going to get out of it?"

"There's no escaping this time," I say, covering my mouth as I chew.

"I guess we're in the same boat. My mom's making me go to the grad party too."

My eyes widen and I heave a small sigh of relief. Charlie and I had a pact to skip the grad dance if possible. We weren't foolish enough to believe we'd be able to get away with skipping out on the graduation ceremony, but we thought the dance would be do-able since we'd already managed to ditch Prom.

"Oh my God, well at least we'll have each other," I say.

"Don't you want a date?"

A pang of desire so strong strikes me that it takes me by surprise. Yes, I want a date and I want that date to be Jon, but this is reality and the reality of my life is that I will be dateless.

27

"No, it's okay. I don't mind going alone. Like I said, we'll have each other," I say, knowing full well Charlie knows I'm lying.

"I told my mother if I have to go then I'm taking a girl," she says, "but I didn't mean you. I meant like in a real date."

She's not smiling and I have a sneaking suspicion she means it. Charlie's sexual orientation is a slippery slope and a road we don't travel down very often.

"You said you had an idea this morning, so what is it?" I ask, changing the subject before things get awkward.

A sly smile unfurls on Charlie's lips and she nods over her shoulder to a table behind us. I know without looking who's sitting there — Nino, Tyler and Julia.

I put down my fork, my appetite vanishing with the sudden anxiety churning in my belly.

"What are you thinking?" I ask with hesitation.

"You've got to practice."

"Whaddaya mean, I have to practice?" I ask flatly. If becoming invisible means I have to endure tons of humiliation and embarrassment, I'm not sure I want to practice, especially if I have to throw myself at the mercy of Nino, Tyler and Julia.

"You've got to learn to control your *ability*," Charlie says.

"That's going to be hard. I mean, look what happened in my room yesterday when I tried to do it on purpose. I was only gone for a split second."

Charlie stabs her fries and crams them into her mouth, then takes a swig of soda to wash them down.

"You've got to do it." Her face shrivels in a look of pain and her hands have curled into fists. "God, I wish I could make myself invisible. Do you know what I'd do to those assholes? I'd make their lives so friggin' miserable, they'd want to go hang themselves, just like they've done to us."

Her pain is reflected in her pale eyes. Charlie's had it worse than me. I'm picked on 'cause of my size and although it hurts like hell, I've got my dreams to pull me through. One day I'll be a famous best-selling novelist and maybe one day I won't be so fat. But everyone sees Charlie like she's some kind of freak, with her tattoo and purple-streaked hair, and the rumors of her being a lesbian and all. She's scrappy and tough and has been in more fights than I can count. But it's taken a toll on her, especially since she's an only child and her mother's always working. I'm pretty much all she's got.

"I will, I'll practice," I tell her and this brings a smile to her face.

"There's no time like the present." She nods again at the shitheads behind us.

"What exactly do you expect me to do?" Panic edges my voice.

"It's time for revenge."

"No," I say in a furious whisper and shake my head, my stomach doing flip-flops. "I'm not ready."

Charlie reaches out and places her hands on both sides of my head and turns my head-shaking "no" to a furious nodding "yes."

I pull away and fix her with a glare.

"Look," she says, leaning closer, "don't they deserve to be punished for what they did to you? Look at them. They think they're better than us."

Reluctantly, my eyes find them. Other kids are now sitting at their table. To my horror, I spot Jon. Nino's holding court again, talking to the huddled group. They laugh at something he says and look my way.

"I think Nino's telling everyone about what they did to me at the park."

"See," Charlie says, "satisfaction reflecting in her eyes. "We've got a great opportunity here. School's almost over, we've got to make them pay while we still can. Let's go to the bathroom. We can practice there."

We choose the bathroom at the other end of the hallway, far from the cafeteria. Thankfully, it's empty and Charlie and I lock ourselves in the handicap stall where we'll have more room. The stench of disinfectant mingles with other more stomach churning scents. I have a strong urge to pull my T-shirt over my nose to keep from gagging and would if I were alone in the graffiti-riddled stall.

"How do you feel right now?" Charlie asks.

Like puking, I think but I know what she means and I say, "Upset."

"Good."

I huff and throw her a look.

"I don't mean that I *want* you to be upset... well, I do, but not because I'm mean. It's just that you've got to bring up the bad feelings if you're gonna vanish, like you did in your bedroom last night. That's the key. But I think, when I reacted, I pulled you out of it. This time, I'll try to be calm, okay?"

"Then what?"

Even though no one else is in the bathroom, Charlie puts her lips to my ear and whispers her plan, slowly drawing a smile from me. I imagine the scene in my mind and a sense of empowerment and satisfaction washes over me. I only hope I have the courage to do what she wants.

"Oh and we've got to find out if you're holding something, if it disappears too. Hold onto your cellphone and I'll keep a close eye on it."

"Good idea." I pull my phone from my pocket and hold it in front of my chest.

My practice session begins in frustration.

"This might take a while," I explain after the first few attempts only result in a split second flicker.

"Don't worry, we'll do this every day, whenever we can find time," Charlie explains. "I was hoping we could do a little something to those bastards today but we'll take it slow until you're ready. We've still got some time."

When the bell rings, indicating lunch is over, I've managed to make myself invisible, cellphone and all, a total of ten times, but never for more than a couple of seconds.

Chapter Eight

All week I practiced my disappearing act. I'm managing longer and longer stretches and my confidence, though still budding, is growing. Of course Charlie has to be with me or I won't know if I've actually disappeared or not. This little problem has me a bit concerned. Since my ability to vanish is becoming stronger and more frequent, I'm worried I might wink out without knowing it. Next month I start driving lessons and I can just imagine disappearing while behind the wheel. How freaked out would my instructor be? Actually, that thought makes me chuckle.

It's Saturday morning and Charlie has come over to help me practice. We don't have much time before my dreaded shopping trip with Mom. But we manage to sneak in a short session in my room.

"You're doing great," Charlie announces excitedly, eyeing the stopwatch in her hand. "You passed the two-minute mark this time."

"That's not long enough to execute the plan," I say and plop down on my bed. Practicing drains me. It's hard on me emotionally, having to drag up and re-live those terrible moments in my life.

"We've still got more time to practice. Just as long as you're making progress and can go for longer and longer stretches, I think we'll be fine."

"I'd like to hit the ten-minute mark. Then I'd be comfortable."

"You'll get there. I'm sure of it. Do you wanna to try again?"

I sigh. "God, no. I need a break."

There's a knock at the door. Charlie quickly opens my desk drawer, throws the stopwatch in and closes it again, before my mother pops her head into the room.

"Hi Charlie," Mom says, and then turns her attention to me. "You ready to go, Lola?"

I'm almost relieved. No more practising today, but the thought of shopping with my mom brings another more horrifying dread to the surface.

"Can Charlie come?" I blurt out and realize my mistake as soon as Mom's eyebrows smash together.

She plasters on a fake smile. "Any other time, I'd love to have Charlie come along, but you know this is supposed to be a mother-daughter thing." She looks at Charlie. "I'm sorry, Hun."

"Oh, no prob, Mrs. Savullo. I've got some things to take care of today, anyway." Charlie throws me a quick look of "aww poor you, I hope you survive" and leaves.

"I'll text you," I call after her.

Mom throws me another look. "No cellphone. It's just you and me this afternoon."

I sigh in resignation and smack my cell down on my desk.

* * * *

The mall is crowded and we've parked about a mile away; at least that's how it feels, as we trudge through the parking lot, dodging water-filled pot holes from the early morning's rain. Just as the sun is breaking through the clouds, and the day is showing promise, I'm stuck in a mall with a seriously addicted shopaholic.

Mom drags me from store to store and makes me try on at least a hundred frilly, sparkly and always uncomfortably tight dresses. She ooohs and ahhhs and finally settles on a hot pink, off-the-shoulder number with lavender sequins.

"Lola, look at you!" she squeals and claps her hands.

The bored-looking salesgirl, who is no older than I am, bolsters her enthusiasm. "Yes, I think this is the one," she says with forced fervor.

"No. I don't like it," I say, but Mom and the salesgirl are discussing me as if I'm not there.

"I've got to get her spiky heels and some bling," says Mom.

"Oh, then you've got to go to Jazzbees for the jewelry and Stance for the shoes. They've got the best selection and the most fashionable..."

"Mom," I interrupt. "I said I don't like this dress." I tried on a black sleeveless with a high collar a few dresses back that I'd kinda liked, but Mom thought it was too plain. "Not enough pizzazz," she'd said.

"Just a sec, Lola, honey." She holds her hand up to me and turns back to the girl. "So, where are those stores? Are they on this level?"

"I want the black one," I protest, but my words fall on deaf ears.

Mom whips out her cellphone and snaps a picture of me in the awful dress. I look like a hooker from 1982.

"What are you doing?" I screech and jump into the change room.

"I just want Eva to see the dress before I make up my mind. I need one more opinion. I'm sending it to her."

"*No!* I'm not getting this one. This is the kind of dress you and Eva would love, it's not for me." I slam the door shut and struggle to free myself from the hideous thing. I put my jeans and T-shirt back on, and step out, determined to get my way.

"Lola?" Mom asks, sounding all weird. "Where'd you go?"

She's looking right at me. "I'm here," I answer.

"Oh, my God, where's my girl. Where did she go?" Mom turns to the salesgirl who simply throws her hands in the air and shrugs.

Mom jumps toward the change room and I instinctively leap out of the way. Anger and frustration must have brought on an episode of invisibility. I realize I didn't have to move. She would have passed right through me anyway, like my hand did that day at the camp when I tried to grab Justine.

A deep satisfaction settles over me as I watch my mother and the salesgirl in their frantic search. I stroll over to a comfy looking chair and sit. It's interesting that I can manage to sit or even bump into things and hurt myself while invisible, but when I try to grab something or someone, my hand passes right through.

I watch for a while longer, as Mom and the salesgirl, whose name I've since discovered is Anna, run around searching for me in the most ridiculous of places. They peer in every change room and even check behind the sales counter and storage room in the back of the store. How on earth would I have gotten from the change room to the storage room without anyone seeing? That is, if I weren't invisible.

The store manager, a tall lanky blonde with a superior attitude picks up the phone and I hear her talking to mall security.

Oh no! I stand, wave my arms and scream at the top of my lungs. It was fun watching Mom get all panicky while looking for me, but I don't need the added drama of a security guard. Then maybe even the cops. "Hey, I'm here. I'm right here."

What if I never come back? There's no doubt I've been gone longer than my past record of a little over two minutes. But exactly how long, I don't know; five, six minutes? My heart bangs against my ribs and I begin to hyperventilate.

"Oh, God, Lola! Where have you been?" Mom cries and wraps her arms around me. I'm met with a face full of hair. With her heels and piled up hair, Mom's almost my height. I squeeze back and let out a long breath of relief. My heart slows, and my breathing becomes regular, but my legs are still a little rubbery.

I've drawn a crowd. Anna and the manager hang back with the shoppers. A low applause erupts from the on-lookers and suddenly I feel a little guilty, not to mention like a five-year-old reunited with her mother after being lost in Wal-Mart.

"Where were you?"

"I was sitting right there the whole time. You haven't been listening to a thing I've said and I suppose you didn't see me because you didn't want to." I feign indignation.

"How in the world could I do that? It wasn't just me looking for you," she replies, confusion settling on her face.

"Well, I was right there." I point to the chair.

"But... but... how in the world...?"

"It doesn't matter, Mom. I'm fine and I'm right here, so can we go back and get the black dress?"

The manager and Anna the salesgirl have gone back to work and the crowd has dissipated. Mom pulls a compact from her purse and applies another coat of lipstick on her collagen-enhanced lips and pats her hair back in place. Settling her nerves seems to include a bit of preening.

"Oh, okay, if that's what you want, honey," she says absently, looking a million miles away.

I smile. "Yeah. That's what I want."

Chapter Nine

Victory is mine. Well, sort of.

I still have to go to the grad dance and I have to wear a friggin' dress, but I suppose I won because Mom bought the one I kinda liked. I shoved it in my closet as soon as we got home, and there it can stay until I absolutely have no choice but to wear it. Mom even relented on the jewelry. My little disappearing act threw enough of a scare into her that she let me get what *I* wanted. All that's left are my shoes, but I convinced her to get them another time. I'm hoping to go to the mall on my own, or with Charlie, to pick them. Shoe shopping with Mom is another nightmare I could do without.

It's Sunday morning and time for my visit with Grandma Rose. I slip out of the house before anyone's up and don't bother to leave a note, figuring they'll know where I am. As I approach the park where I was almost beaten up a week ago, I quicken my pace, even though no one's there at this hour. I keep my gaze trained straight ahead, completely ignoring the corner of Whiteside and Moorehouse. The heat of humiliation flushes my cheeks and I fight back tears as I remember what they did to me, and that Jon was there to witness it.

By the time I get to Gran's and slip the key into the lock of her apartment door, I realize I'd clenched my jaw the whole way over, causing an uncomfortable ache. With thumbs, I rub at the place where the bones meet, trying to unlock the tension there.

"Is that my darling granddaughter?" Gran calls from her usual spot in the solarium.

My spirits lift when I hear her voice and I abandon my massage. Gran's company is all I'll need to help me relax. "Hi, Grandma Rose," I answer, making my way over to have a look at her latest creation.

"Do you like it?" she asks, grinning from ear to ear.

I'm faced with an unrecognizable blob of paint vaguely in the shape of a human face. My eyes search frantically for the photo Gran inevitably uses while painting, and find nothing.

"I did this one out of my imagination," she proclaims proudly. "I think I've gotten good enough to not need a picture."

"Yeah, Gran, you did a great job," I lie.

"Guess who it is."

"Um." I quickly search my mental database for Gran's favorite entertainers, but I can't even tell if she's painted a man or a woman.

"Frank Sinatra," I say, knowing he's her all-time favorite.

Gran's smile goes out and her shoulders slump. "Aw, hell. It's Katy Perry. I painted it for you 'cause I know you like her."

"That would have been my second guess. Most definitely, as a matter of fact, I was going to guess Katy Perry but…"

Grandma raises a paint-speckled hand and laughs. "It's okay, Kiddo. This one stinks. I guess the best place for it's the garbage chute at the end of the hall." She takes it from the easel and starts for the door.

"No," I say quickly. "Leave it. When it's dry, I'll take it home."

She narrows her eyes. "You sure?"

"Absolutely! I'll hang it over my bed."

"Okay," she says, swinging it back onto the easel. "It'll take a day or two to dry. I used oils this time."

I sniff the air and turn in the direction of the kitchen. "Is something burning?"

"Oh, shit!" Gran rushes past me to the kitchen and pulls open the oven door.

I follow her in time to see a pan of charcoal black disks, smoking and crumbling.

"Damn it. I wanted to make your favorite cookies. You know, the ones you just have to slice and plop on the pan. The *foolproof*, a monkey can bake 'em ones."

Grandma Rose isn't much of a baker and the only two dishes I've ever seen her cook were pasta with tomato sauce from a jar, and Shake 'n Bake chicken wings.

"It's okay. I shouldn't be eating cookies anyway. Mom just bought me a new dress for grad and I have to be able to fit into it next month," I say, patting my belly.

Grandma throws the pan, burned up cookies and all, into the sink and turns on the water. A black river runs off it and down the drain.

"Lola, don't you worry about your figure. That's your mom talking."

We move into the living room and sit. I find my usual corner of the couch and Gran settles in the armchair across from me. The room is small and cluttered, but I find it cosy. Family pictures are everywhere and most of them are of me. I know I'm her favorite without her ever having said so.

"I know I'm fat. I'm a big, fat giant. Look at you. I'm not like you. I'm not like Mom, or Eva or anyone else in the family except Dad's Uncle Sammy," I say emphatically.

"Lola!" Gran says, like I'm in trouble. "Stop it right now. I don't like hearing you talk about yourself that way." She rests a gnarled hand on my knee. "Stop hating yourself, honey. It hurts my heart."

I take a deep breath to keep from crying and clutch her hand. "I just want to be like everyone else. I want to be pretty and have lots of friends and... a boyfriend." My gaze darts away and settles on the floor.

She lifts my chin with a finger. "You will. Don't you worry. You've got your whole life ahead of you." Gran bites her bottom lip and I can tell she wants to say something else. She turns away, and then looks back at me out of the corner of her eye.

I lean forward in anticipation. But she just squeezes my hand and smiles.

"Gran? What were you going to say?"

"Huh?"

"It looked like you wanted to tell me something."

She gives me another contemplative look and sighs. "Has anything… out of the ordinary happened to you lately?"

"Like?"

"Oh, I don't know, just anything that may seem impossible, but it's happening anyway?" she says quickly, then studies my expression.

I freeze. *Is she talking about what I think she's talking about?*

Chapter Ten

"Lola, honey," Grandma explains, "out of our whole family, you and I are the most alike. Now, we may not be the same size, but we definitely look like we're related. You've got dark curly hair like I have or *used* to." She laughs. "And blue eyes. I'm you in miniature. I'm a heck of a lot shorter but I've got the same sturdiness to me. It's your mom and Eva who are different. They're your Grandpa Ken all the way, so fine boned and delicate. Did you know that you and I even have the same blood type?" She cocks a brow.

"No. I don't even know what my blood type is. How do you know we've got the same blood?"

Gran grins. "It was the first thing I asked when you were born. You're A-negative just like me. You and I are the only ones in the family with that type of blood besides your great-great-grandmother Nell. She was my grand-mother and she had it too. It's very rare, ya know."

"Ahhh," I say, wondering where this is all going.

"It first happened to me right around your age," Grandma Rose says with a nod. "I suspect it's happened to you by now too. It's all right, you can tell me." Gran's eyes are huge as she gazes hopefully at me.

I hug myself tight around my middle and decide to tell her, only I'm hoping we're talking about the same thing and that she's not just asking if I've gotten my period by now or something.

"You're talking about *vanishing*, right?" I cringe a little, bracing for her reply.

"Oh, heavens, yes. So it's happened!" Gran is on her feet, doing a little happy dance. "I knew it would. I just knew it!"

An overwhelming sense of relief washes over me and I smile. "How did you know?"

"Because you're like me. Didn't you hear what I just told you? We've got the same blood, Lola, the same DNA."

"You mean, you can disappear too?" My heart quickens.

"Well, no, not any more, but I did when I was younger. I had a name for it. I called it The Vanishing."

"The Vanishing," I repeat. I like the sound of that. "So then The Vanishing will eventually go away?"

"It did for me and I suspect when the time is right, it will for you, too."

I purse my lips and nod slowly, contemplating what Gran's just told me. My ability's so new. I'm not quite sure how I feel about it yet. It's a pain in the ass and can scare the crap outta me, but I would be sad to see it go so soon, especially now that I'm gaining a little control over it. I wouldn't want to deal with it forever, though, so Gran's words are reassuring.

I pull my legs up under me and make myself comfortable. There's much to learn about The Vanishing and I want to know it all. "So, tell me about when it first happened to you. How old were you? Where were you? What were you doing? Is there any way to control it?"

Grandma Rose holds up both hands. "Slow your roll there, honey. We've got all afternoon." She gets to her feet and pulls me from my comfy corner of the couch. "Come on, let's walk and talk."

* * * *

"I can't believe it, Gran, why didn't you tell me sooner? It would have been nice to know what to expect, ya know," I say as we circle the track around the small man-made lake at the end of her apartment complex.

Grandma giggles. "Now, how would that have sounded? 'Lola, one day you'll simply vanish, but don't worry, you'll return to the visible spectrum, *eventually*.' It woulda scared ya too much. Besides, I didn't know for sure that it would happen to you."

I strip off my jacket and tie it around my waist. The warmth of the late spring sun feels good on my face. "Well, then why did you bring it up now?"

"Funny thing is, I saw it on your face."

Fooling Grandma Rose is near impossible. She always knows how I feel. Maybe that's in the DNA too.

I give Gran the details of my first experience and then tell her about the times after. I tell her how I practice with Charlie and that I've been able to vanish for longer and longer periods.

"Good for you, honey. You're a smart girl and you're doing all the right things. Practising is great. Keep it up."

"And yesterday, I vanished on Mom at the mall. I must have been gone close to five minutes. Oh, my God, Gran, I wish you could've seen. She was making me try on hideous dresses and it was friggin' humiliating. When I disappeared, she went nuts. The salesgirl, the manager and Mom were running all over that store looking for me in the most ridiculous of places, and I was right there in front of them the whole time."

She laughs so hard, tears spring to her eyes. "I do wish I could have seen that!"

I slip my hand into her bony knuckled one, her still vibrantly creative one and we continue to talk and walk.

"There's something I've been wondering about. How come I can sit in a chair and even manage to hurt myself, but when I try to touch someone or something, my hand passes right through?"

Gran's lips thin down in contemplation. "Just a mystery of The Vanishing, I guess." She shrugs. "I never did figure that one out for myself."

A faint breeze wafts over us, bringing with it the smells of spring. I take a deep contented breath, feeling safe and loved and grateful. "Tell me about the first time it happened to you."

"Ha!" Gran laughs. My question obviously brings up a noteworthy memory. "The first time I disappeared, I was about to kiss a boy," Gran says. "I was sixteen-and-a-half and Chuck Hutchins, my boyfriend at the time, had just walked me home after a date. We got to my porch and he leaned in for a smooch and *poof*, I was gone." Grandma chuckles. "The poor boy started to cry and ran home. We never did go out on another date."

I double over with laughter, picturing the scene and when my laughing fit's over, she tells me stuff, good stuff.

"Have you figured out how to tell when you're invisible yet?" she asks.

I whip my head toward her, all ears. "There's a way to tell?"

"Yes, it's subtle, though, so you'll have to pay attention to the signs your body gives you. When you're invisible, your heartbeat slows right down, but only for a moment. It's as if it's barely beating. But when you're about to vanish, there's a little flutter in your chest. The same thing happens when you're about to return."

"I was too freaked out to notice anything. But this is good to know, Gran. I'll pay attention next time."

"Yes, you do that. You'll soon know the signs. Hungry? You want to grab something to eat?"

"No." I don't want our conversation to end. I'm still too full of questions.

"Okay, just let me know when you get hungry," she says, slowing her pace and pressing a finger to her neck. "Heart's beating a little fast."

Suddenly, I realize I'm being selfish, that *she* might be tired or hungry. "Are you tired? 'Cause we can stop. Or if you're hungry..."

She waves me off. "Naw, I'm fine. Just need to slow down a bit."

I slow my pace to match hers. "How about Uncle Brian, can he do it?" Uncle Brian is Grandma Rose's son, my mother's brother.

Gran shakes her head. "No, none of the men can."

"So only the women in the family?"

"Yup, and it comes from the Irish side. I was afraid your dad's Italian genes would mess you up like it did Eva, but thankfully you've got more Irish in ya than Italian." She winks.

Grandpa Ken was English, but Grandma Rose is 100% Irish and proud of it. I always thought of myself as a mutt, a little of this and a little of that, but now that Gran has explained where The Vanishing comes from, it's like I suddenly belong somewhere and feel closer to her than ever.

"When did The Vanishing stop for you?" I ask.

Gran waves a hand in the air. "I dunno for sure. I guess when the menopause hit."

"Wow, so it stayed for quite a while?"

"I suppose it stayed for as long as it needed to." She heaves a sigh.

"What if it happens because I'm wishing it to?" I ask, thinking of Charlie's theory. "Because if you think about it, it happens when I'm either scared or embarrassed and desperately wishing I could blend into the woodwork."

"Hmmm, well, I suppose that could be partly right. But I really can't say for sure because it's happened when I was really happy too. Your great-great-grandmother Nell told me that any strong emotion triggers it. Whether it's happiness or sadness, it doesn't matter."

That makes sense, since it happened to Gran when she was about to kiss a boy. Oh, great, now I have to worry about being too happy or excited. What if I disappear when a boy tries to kiss me!

"But one thing I do know for sure," she continues, "is that the ability to disappear is a gift. A great and wonderful gift."

"It's gotten me out of a few tight spots, so I guess, in a way, it is a gift."

"Lola, you have no idea just how powerful a gift it is. You just wait and see."

It's nice to know that I'm not alone and not some kind of freak, after all. I squint and smile up at the sun warming my body, lulling me into a blissful cocoon of contentment. Then I look at Grandma Rose and wish with all my might that she could live forever.

"One more lap and we'll call it a day, Kiddo," Gran says with a wink.

And off we go, hand in hand.

If only time would stand still.

Chapter Eleven

Can u meet me at Tim Horton's? I text Charlie.

Half a second later, her reply reads, *B there in 5*.

After my day with Gran, I'm anxious to fill her in on the new stuff I've learned.

I'm so excited I practically fly to the coffee shop. When Charlie ambles in, I'm tucked away at our usual table in the corner, nursing a large orange pekoe and nibbling a peanut butter cookie.

Charlie grabs a large double double coffee and a chocolate dip donut before settling down across from me. "How was Gran?" she asks and grins. "Did you tell her about your super power?"

"Yup, and she can do it, too, or at least she used to be able to. She even has a name for it."

Charlie's eyes flash with interest and she nearly chokes on her donut. "No way!" she says, pounding on her chest and coughing.

"Yes, *way*." I smile, enjoying her reaction. I lean close. "She calls it The Vanishing," I say in an excited whisper.

Charlie covers my hand with hers. "That's friggin' unbelievable. It's great news for you. It must run in the family."

I explain about the A-negative blood and the Irish thing and then fill her in on everything else Grandma Rose told me.

"Wow, Lola, this is what we needed to hear – there's a way to control it."

"And we're already doing all the right things by practising." I take a long sip of tea and open my mouth to continue when Jon walks in, his laptop tucked under an arm. He grabs what looks like a cherry slushie and settles at the other end of the coffee shop.

It's a quiet afternoon and, aside from us, there are only two other people in the place — an elderly couple enjoying donuts and coffee.

"What's with you?" Charlie follows my wide-eyed gaze. "Oh," she says when she spots Jon.

"I guess he's doing homework," I say absently. My heart races and I push away my tea. No more caffeine for me. "Let's get out of here."

Charlie grabs my arm, pinning me in my seat.

"I've got a better idea," she says. A mischievous smile lights her face.

"Oh, no." I shake my head. "I don't like the look on your face."

"Just listen." She leans close. "I don't think he's seen us yet. Now would be a good time to practice your *skill.*"

"Uh-uh, no way."

"Chicken. This place is practically empty. No one will see you vanish. It's a golden opportunity. Make yourself disappear and walk up to him. Just to see if you can do it. How will you be able to carry out the plan if you don't practice? And I don't mean in the safety of your bedroom."

I think about when I vanished at the mall and how exciting it was. It was a little scary, though, thinking I wouldn't return; but at the same time, I'd never felt more powerful in my entire life.

I eye Jon again. His back is to us and he's busy tapping away on his laptop.

"Oh, God, Charlie, I don't know." My voice quivers.

"I dare you."

I suck in a deep breath. Charlie's right, this is a great way to test things out. There's a tremble in my hands and a rumble in my stomach. If this keeps up, I just might wink out on my own anyway.

48

"Okay," I relent. "But I'm just walking up to him. I'll take a look at what he's working on and report back to you. Okay?"

She nods enthusiastically. I close my eyes.

"Think of the time ..." Charlie begins and my eyes snap open. I fix her with a look that says "shut up."

"Okay, I guess you know what to do," she huffs and leans back to watch.

Eyes closed, I begin again. I try a different tactic and picture Jon pulling me to his chest, tilting his head and kissing me. I can almost feel his lips on mine. A smile tugs at the corners of my mouth because it feels so real. My heart flutters and my eyes fly open. My heart fluttered!

Charlie's jumping excitedly in her seat. I must have done it. I must be invisible. I wave a hand an inch from her face to make certain and, sure enough, she's unflinching. Before I lose my nerve, I push to my feet and make my way over to Jon.

As I close in, I catch his scent. God, he smells good, like soap and freshly shampooed hair mixed with a hint of cologne. I'm there now, right behind him, and I peer over his shoulder to read what's he's writing. It looks like a story. Oh, wow, he likes to write too! I try to read it, but can't get past the first sentence, distracted by how near I am.

I slide in beside him and our knees brush. The spunk in me comes up because I know he can't feel my leg touching his, and so I stay close. My whole body tingles. With exquisite slowness, I lift a hand to his hair and swear I can feel my fingers passing through his thick shaggy mane. He's oblivious, still working on his story. Inching even closer, I settle my head on his shoulder and, with eyes closed, I inhale him. Contentment washes over me. I could stay like this forever.

Jon screams and leaps away. His eyes round with what looks like fear.

I jump, knocking my knee against the table. The slushie bounces, but doesn't spill.

"Where did you come from?" he hollers.

Bile threatens to rise and I'm terrified I'm going to hurl. "I'm sorry," I manage to say before running from the coffee shop. A moment later, Charlie's sprinting up behind me, calling breathlessly for me to stop.

I do and now I'm crying. What a fool I've made of myself. I had my head on his shoulder! I'll never be able to face him again. But he sits right in front of me in homeroom. How will I escape that?

Charlie pulls me into a hug. "I'm sorry. The whole thing was my fault. I'm so sorry."

"Can we keep going?" I say, wanting to put as much distance as I can between me and the place where I've just royally humiliated myself.

"Sure. Why don't we go to my house?" Charlie suggests. "My mom's at work and we can talk."

Charlie lives with her mom in a small townhouse a couple blocks away from me. Her parents have been divorced for years, and I've only seen her dad a handful of times since then. Her mother works two jobs just to make ends meet. Charlie has a part-time job at the grocery store and helps out as much as she can, and more than likely she'll have to get a full-time job after graduating high school. That really sucks for her. I know how much she wants to go to art school.

We walk in silence, arm-in-arm. Nothing needs to be said. She's my best friend and, right now, I just need to be with her.

We settle in Charlie's place, which is in the basement. The townhouse is a two bedroom, but Charlie has taken over the entire bottom level as her lair. She decorated it herself. There's a bedroom area, a bathroom with a small shower, a living room complete with a love seat and a television and even a tiny refrigerator, but no kitchen.

Three of the walls are painted red and one is black. Her artwork fills the entire back wall where her living room is. There are posters, mostly of heavy metal and grunge bands that give me the creeps, especially the ones of Marilyn Manson and Rob Zombie. Yuck! But Charlie loves them. Then there's the poster of Megan Fox striking a sexy, pouty pose: that one I ignore and don't ask questions about. Charlie is who Charlie is, and I love her no matter what.

"Wanna soda?" she asks, opening the mini-fridge.

"No thanks." I plop dejected onto the love seat. "What have I done?" I lower my head into my hands.

Charlie sits beside me and rubs my knee. "God, I feel awful. But I thought you were just going to have a peek over his shoulder and that was all. I didn't think you'd …"

"No, don't say it." I raise a hand to stop her. "Please, I just want to wash the memory away."

"Okay, okay, but it was kinda funny. You shoulda seen the look on his face."

My eyes meet hers reluctantly and I can't help myself. I laugh.

Soon, we're both laughing so hard we're doubled over.

"Stop, stop," I say between fits of laughter. My stomach muscles ache and tears roll down my cheeks. After what feels like a small forever, we settle down.

"Oh God, I'm going to have to see him in homeroom tomorrow," I say.

A smile plays on Charlie's lips as if she's still trying to rein in her laughter, but when her eyes meet mine, she clears her throat and her expression becomes solemn. She taps a finger to her lips, as if considering my options. "Why not just pretend like it never happened?" she says finally.

"Oh, come on!"

"Maybe he'll think it was his imagination."

I remember the day in the park when I vanished. I don't think Jon actually saw me disappear, but the reality is, first I was there and then I was gone.

"I doubt that. He's gonna think I'm some kind of freak. And maybe I am."

"Don't even say that. You're not a freak. I think it's so cool that you can disappear." Charlie tilts her head in an attempt to catch my gaze. "Besides, I bet he doesn't even bring it up. What's he gonna say?"

"Well, whether he brings it up or not, I don't have much choice. I've got to go to school."

"It's already the end of May, whatta we got, another four weeks? I think you can stick it out 'til then." She offers a hopeful smile.

"And then I'll never see him again," I say, and tears sting my eyes.

Chapter Twelve

I wake with a start. School today. The thought sends my heart off in a sprint and my stomach into flip-flops. I roll out of bed and grab my cellphone.

I'm nervous, I text Charlie.

A second later, she replies, *Don't worry, I'm here 4 u.*

It's great to know my best friend will be by my side, but a knot of worry tightens in my belly and steals my appetite. I skip breakfast and wait for Charlie at the end of my street.

When she arrives, we walk in silence. There's nothing to say to make things better any way.

Maple Ridge Secondary School looms menacingly ahead. My legs feel like they weigh a hundred pounds each, and with every step, I creep closer to the inevitable – my certain mortification.

"Am I still here?" I ask.

"Yeah," Charlie answers. "Why? You feelin' like you might wink out?"

"I'm so friggin' nervous. You never know."

"Try some deep breathing."

I do as she suggests, pulling in long, slow breaths and letting them out with controlled measure. Remarkably, I feel a little better.

"Keep your head held high." Charlie gives my hand a squeeze as we make our way through the front doors.

I think I'm just being paranoid, but it feels like all eyes are on me, as Charlie and I walk to my locker. Maybe it has something to do with the fact I'm sucking in lungfulls of air and looking like I'm about to faint.

"Stay cool. You'll make it through this," she says, brushing my hand with a finger. "I have to go, but I'll see you at lunch."

Charlie leaves but halfway down the hall turns and gives me a thumbs up. I smile half-heartedly, grab my books from my locker and hyperventilate all the way to class. The whole time, praying I don't vanish.

Homeroom never felt more ominous. Jon is here already. I slide into my seat as silently as a shadow. My eyes are glued to the back of his head in anticipation of movement.

He turns.

I jump.

"How did you do that?" he asks excitedly. His eyes are wide and smiling.

A slow ease washes over me and I return his smile. "Do what?" I ask, even though I know full well what he's referring to.

"Disappear," he whispers and leans closer.

I open my mouth to reply, but Mrs. Wright has walked in and throws a "time to stop chatting" look our way.

"Can I sit with you at lunch?" he asks.

I feel my cheeks flush and for a moment I'm terrified my heart will flutter. As nonchalantly as possible, I suck in a few deep breaths and manage to calm myself. The look on Jon's face lets me know I'm still within the visible spectrum.

"Sure," I say, hoping he doesn't hear the wobble in my voice. Both excitement and fear race through me.

When class is finally over, I walk out as quickly as possible without breaking into a full run, so Jon won't have time to ask any more questions. Thank God Charlie will be with me at lunch as a buffer.

The rest of the morning passes much too quickly and, before I know it, the lunch bell rings. I wait for Charlie at her locker instead of meeting her at our usual table in the cafeteria.

Her familiar form heading down the hall brings a relieved smile to my lips.

"How'd it go?" she asks.

"Actually, pretty good." Now my smile is huge. "He's having lunch with us."

"What?"

"He wants to know what happened and we couldn't talk in class."

"So he wasn't freaked out?"

"No, he looked..." I pause, searching for the right word. "Fascinated."

"Wow. That's great... I guess, but do you think you should tell him? I mean, look who he's been hanging around with lately."

I exhale like I've been punched in the gut. Why didn't I think of that?

"We better go, he'll be waiting," I say. "I'll play it by ear. If I don't get a good vibe, I won't say much."

"I don't think you should say anything," Charlie warns as we head to the cafeteria.

More than anything, I want to explain myself to Jon. I don't want him to think I'm a weirdo. But Charlie's right. I have to be careful.

Jon waves and smiles as we enter the cafeteria. I smile back and quicken my step, but Charlie catches my wrist and holds tight.

"Be cool," she whispers.

We sit side by side across from Jon.

"Hey," Jon says, eyeing Charlie.

She nods. Her lips remain a tight, thin line.

Jon turns his attention to me. I can tell he wasn't expecting Charlie to be with me.

There's an awkward silence as we fish out our respective lunches and start to eat.

"So, um, you gonna tell me what happened yesterday?" Jon says finally, between bites.

I set down my fork and push my leftover stir-fry aside. I'm too nervous to eat. I cast a quick glance at Charlie who's watching Jon through narrowed eyes.

"How can we trust you?" Charlie asks flatly. "You're friends with those assholes." She tips her head toward the rowdy table.

"Oh, no, not really." Jon throws his hands up to drive the point home. "My buddy Mark, you know Mark Granski? He moved away last month. I was trying to make new friends. You know how it is? I've known those guys since kindergarten. They're not all that bad."

I try to put myself in Jon's shoes and give him the benefit of the doubt. I hadn't realized he was so tight with Mark and it makes sense that he would try to find new friends. But Nino and Tyler?

"Ah, yeah, they are. They're dickheads," Charlie snarls.

I throw her a look. She doesn't have to be so mean right off the bat. Maybe he's not friends with them any more. "You still hanging out with Nino and Tyler?" I ask tentatively.

Jon clears his throat. His leg shakes up and down in a nervous bob that sends a tremor through the table. "Sort of."

"Don't tell him shit." Charlie crosses her arms.

Red spots burn on his cheeks and he turns to Charlie. "You know what. This is between Lola and me."

The words were said out of anger, but I can't help it. I love hearing him say "Lola and me." A goofy smile crosses my lips.

"What are you smiling about?" Charlie asks.

With pleading eyes, I say in a harsh whisper, "Just let me tell him, please."

"It's your funeral," she replies and turns away.

My head is telling me not to, but my heart is in the driver's seat right now. And before I can stop myself, the words flow.

Charlie gives her head a slow shake.

I tell Jon everything.

Chapter Thirteen

Charlie scoots her chair out of the way, giving me center stage. Jon listens. His mouth hangs open like a gate on a busted hinge.

No one interrupts and the words flow from me in a torrent. I try not to let emotion get in the way and just speak until there's nothing left to say.

"So, that's it," I say finally, but made sure to change the real reason for why Jon found me with my head resting on his shoulder. "Charlie dared me," I said, which was partially true anyway.

Jon's frozen, eyes round with wonder and his jaw still lax.

"You gonna say something, or are you just gonna sit there looking stupid?" Charlie asks.

He snaps from his stupor with a shake of his head. "I know you're telling the truth. I saw it with my own eyes," he says, as if trying to convince himself.

"Well, yeah," Charlie snaps, "she's telling the truth."

"You disappeared that day at the park too, didn't you?" he asks, ignoring Charlie. "Wow, wow, wow. This is friggin' crazy." He slaps a palm on the table.

I beam. I've impressed him.

"But you can't say anything to anyone, okay?" I give him my best pleading eyes and Charlie throws in a glare.

"No! Of course not." He crosses his heart.

"Of course not what?" Nino says, clamping a hand on Jon's shoulder.

I jolt. He seemed to come out of nowhere.

"Nothin' man," Jon says, wincing as Nino tightens his grip.

"Bullshit! Spill." Nino pulls out a chair and, to my horror, he sits with us at our table.

I peer past him and see Tyler and Julia smiling at the unfolding scene.

"Let's go," Charlie says, getting to her feet.

"Yeah, why don't you and your girlfriend get the hell outta here. No freaks allowed." Nino's lips twist into a cruel grin.

My eyes fill with tears and heat spreads from my chest to my neck and into my cheeks.

"Go on, ya fat dyke. Go with your girlfriend."

Charlie slams a fist to the table. "Asshole," she snarls, grabs my wrist and pulls me away.

I barely make it out of the cafeteria before the tears spill. Charlie shoulders open the front doors and suddenly we're outside. The sun feels good and I breathe in fresh air while wiping my wet eyes with a shirtsleeve.

"Same shit, different day," Charlie says.

"Then why am I not used to it yet?"

We walk around to the other side of the school and settle under a large, old oak.

"Don't let Nino get to you. He's a loser and a bully." Then a smile sweeps across her face. "Think of our plan."

I try to find some delight in her words and in "the plan," but Nino scares the shit out of me and I'm not so sure I can carry it out any more. It's a great fantasy; a diversion and maybe that's all it is. Nino's won. He always wins. All the girls love him and all the guys want to hang with him. And what am I? I'm a pathetic slob who hates herself so much, I can actually make myself into what I, and everyone else thinks I am, an invisible nothing.

"I think we should forget about it. I can't pull it off," I say. What was left of my confidence is now shattered.

Charlie lurches forward and grabs my hands. "Don't crap out on this. It's our chance to get even."

"It's not the right time to talk about this, Char."

"Okay, we'll let it be for now, but I won't let you back out." She wags a finger and fixes me with a stern look.

I nod, not wanting to argue. There's something more important on my mind. "Why didn't he leave?" I sigh.

"Jon? I guess he's an asshole too. I told you not to tell him anything."

My stomach twists around a knot of worry. *Why did I trust him?*

"There you are."

I whip my head around at the sound of Jon's voice.

"Shit," Charlie snarls under her breath.

His eyes lock on mine. "I'm so sorry."

How do I respond? I could say "it's okay" but it isn't. Why didn't he walk out when Charlie and I did? But he answers my thoughts before I have to put them into words.

"He wouldn't let go. I wanted to come with you guys, but Nino stopped me."

"If you wanted to come," Charlie says, "you would have come. Don't give us that shit."

"No, really, I tried, but he grabbed me – put me in a headlock. Mr. Hollingsworth had to come to my rescue. Look." He pulls his shirt down to reveal an angry red rash. "Bastard," he mutters.

Jon adjusts his collar and kneels beside me. "Are you okay?"

I nod but for some reason the tears come again.

"Please don't cry." His voice is soft and his eyes are kind. "Nino's not worth it."

I'm not crying over Nino. I'm crying because Jon cares.

The lunch bell rings. Jon helps me to my feet and I realize it's the first time I've actually touched him, with my real body, not my invisible one. A little thrill rushes through me.

"Thanks."

"You're a really special girl," he says. "I mean special in a good way," he adds quickly and a blush mounts in his cheeks. His gaze falls to the ground. "You're different from other girls."

Though Charlie is there beside us, for a moment it feels like we're alone as we make our way back inside.

"'Bye," Charlie huffs and peels off in the direction of her next class.

"See you after school," I call after her and wave.

Jon walks me to my locker. The whole time my heart pounds so hard I hear the blood whooshing in my ears. To stay grounded, I take deep breaths – in through the nose and out through my mouth.

After I open my locker, I expect Jon to leave, but to my surprise and delight, he's still here. He leans against the open door, wearing a goofy grin.

"Do you want to go out sometime?"

I freeze. My voice abandons me.

My heart flutters.

"Lola?"

My pulse slows for a moment – I'm gone.

Jon reaches out to the spot he saw me last and his hand passes through me. A jolt of energy jabs into me, like I've stuck my finger in a light socket.

"Lola?" he whispers. "You there? It's okay, I'll just wait here 'til you come back." His eyes dart furtively from one side to the other. He's keeping watch for me; so no one will notice I've vanished.

This puts me at ease. Actually, it does more than that, it makes me happy to know he's protecting me and, a moment later, I'm back.

"Wow, Lola. You're *so* cool! God, I wish I could do that."

"Shhh." I bring a finger to my lips. "Do you think anyone saw?"

"No, nobody noticed. I'm sure of it." His voice hushes to a whisper, "Where did you go?"

I furrow my brow and shrug. "I don't think I actually go anywhere. I could hear you talking and I could see you."

"So cool."

"I gotta learn to control it better," I say more to myself than Jon. I'm starting to worry that The Vanishing is happening more frequently.

"But you told me if you remain calm, you'll be okay. So you just have to be calm," Jon offers.

"Yeah, but how do I do that? That's the hard part."

"I think you just need to know how really great you are and then everything will fall into place." He puts a hand on my arm. "You're the smartest girl I know and I wish you could see what I see."

A smile wants to bloom on my lips, but it would have been better if he'd said I was the most *beautiful* girl he knew.

"And you're talented," he adds. "I know about your writing."

I give him a weak smile and he leans in close. I breathe in his cologne and have an overwhelming urge to caress his cheek.

"And I think you're pretty too."

Now I smile for real.

"I work Saturday night, but do you want to catch a movie with me Sunday?"

I nod. Now it's me with the big goofy grin.

Chapter Fourteen

For the rest of the week I feel as if I'm floating. Jon meets me at my locker every morning and walks with me to homeroom. He even eats lunch with Charlie and me, outside under the oak tree. It's fast becoming "our place" after we decide to steer clear of the cafeteria for a while. Charlie huffs and sighs and I can tell she's not happy with the additional company. She continues to try to convince me I shouldn't trust Jon, but my instincts tell me otherwise. I think she's jealous because of all the attention he's giving me. *Oh well, she's just going to have to get used to it.*

Today's Saturday and I spend most of it working on my story for the competition, but its slow going. I just can't find the motivation and I spend hours staring at a blank page. My mind drifts. I can't stop thinking about Jon and the things he said to me – that I'm pretty and smart. It makes goose flesh rise on my arms. I'm almost embarrassed. No one's ever said those words to me, except for Gran, and I don't think her opinion counts because she's my grandmother and she has no choice.

I wonder what Jon's writing about. I didn't get much of a look when I tried to spy on him at the coffee shop. I'll have to ask him tomorrow if he's going to enter a story for the scholarship award. A contented smile spreads across my face. My dream's coming true. I'm actually going on a date with Jon Kingsbury!

The temptation to call Gran to tell her my awesome news is almost unbearable, but I decide to wait for tomorrow's visit, so I can see her reaction.

I finally pulled a few ideas out of my preoccupied brain and hurriedly got them down on paper. I tuck my story away and rummage through my closet for something to wear on my date tomorrow. Something slimming, probably something black. I decide on my new dark wash jeans and then sneak into Eva's room to root around for a top.

My heart sinks when the unmistakable sound of footsteps stop me cold. I've been caught red-handed.

"What are you doing?" she asks at the door, hands planted firmly on her hips.

"I need to borrow a top."

"What for? You only wear T-shirts."

"I have a date."

Eva laughs. "Yeah right. That's about as likely as one of my tops actually fitting you."

"You might have something…"

She slams a palm inches from my face. "Don't want to hear it. Get out."

I feel my face redden and I throw her a nasty look. I step toward her and she jumps out of the way.

Yeah, that's right. I could pound your little ass into the ground.

Satisfied, I stomp away. Sometimes, being big has its advantages.

The thought of asking for Mom's help flits briefly through my mind, but I let the idea slip away. An impromptu shopping trip is always a possibility, or God forbid, she might actually find something of hers that fits me. I can imagine it, sparkly and low cut. Eva's wardrobe isn't that much different than Mom's, but her taste is slightly less showy. Besides, I don't want Mom to know I have a date. She'll get all nosy. Panic rises; I hope Eva doesn't say anything. But I know my sister well. She's either already forgotten about my date or doesn't believe me anyway, and is immersed again in her own shallow life.

Once back in my room for another round of rummaging, I finally settle on one of my nicer T-shirts. It's fairly new and the colors are right – black and dark gray: slimming colors. It's got long sleeves so it probably doesn't really qualify as a real T-shirt, but it's light enough to wear at this time of year. Besides, Jon likes me the way I am, so why change now? I wince. Only a small part of me really believes that.

* * * *

Finally, it's Sunday morning. I lie here trying to relax and push away the thoughts that are forcing me out of the comfort of my bed. I'm not really nervous about my date with Jon, at least not yet. More than anything, I'm excited, but my adrenaline is definitely pumping. I'm getting used to him, *I think*. Our conversations are never awkward and he's funny, but Charlie's usually there as a buffer. Tonight will be different. It'll just be me and Jon. An uncomfortable churning in my belly finally drives me from my bed.

Hurriedly I dress, pulling on the same clothes I wore the day before. I'll have a shower and wash my hair when I get back from Gran's.

Dad's at the kitchen table, sipping from his giant mug of coffee while scrolling through something on his cellphone. No doubt he'll be heading to the garage for a smoke soon, taking his coffee with him. He's got a nice little set up out there; a couch, a small television and a beer fridge. Mom doesn't allow smoking in the house. She's a reformed smoker and is constantly on Dad's case about quitting. I don't blame her. He smells like an ashtray.

"Good morning," he says brightly when I enter the kitchen.

He's got a few days' growth of stubble and his hair stands stiffly on end; too much gel and hairspray. I cringe at the thought of how many other dads use more hair products than their daughters. Two large hoop earrings adorn his lobes and he's wearing a True Religion shirt and jeans with holes in them. He paid extra for the holes I think.

"Hey, Dad. Mom still asleep?" I pull a bowl from the cupboard and fill it with Cheerios.

"Yeah. She needs her beauty sleep." He grins, looking up from his iPhone. "Going to Gran's today?"

I sit and pour milk into my bowl. "That's the plan."

He puts his phone down and leans on his forearms to scrutinize me. His brows knit in confusion and he gives his head a little shake. "Why, Lola? She's what, seventy-eight, seventy-nine? Why do you want to hang out with an old lady?"

"She's eighty and she's cool," I say. Defiance edges my voice. "I love Grandma Rose."

He laughs. "I know you love her. We all love her. But only you could find an eighty-year-old woman cool. It's the weekend, it's almost summer. Why don't you go out with some friends? You're starting to worry me."

"Don't worry about me." I stare into my cereal.

"But always with the books and the writing." He lifts my face with a finger, which is crowned with black nail polish. "I just want you to be happy."

I sigh and turn away. *How many times do I have to hear this speech?* "You just don't get it. You, Mom, Eva, you're all alike. I'm the outsider in this family. Dad, I am happy. I love to read, I love to write and I love to hang out with Grandma Rose. Why can't you just let me be me? I won't ever be like you guys." I scrape my chair back and stand. "I don't *want* to be like you guys."

I shovel a huge scoop of cereal into my mouth and mumble, "Be back after lunch."

Chapter Fifteen

My mood lifts as soon as I see Grandma Rose's smiling face.

"Keep your shoes on, Kiddo, we're goin' out today," she announces with enthusiasm when I walk through the door. Her make-up is on, her hair is neatly combed and sprayed into place – I can tell by the sheen – and she's dressed in her favorite comfy-looking velour track suit. She shrugs a giant purse onto a shoulder. "Let's go!"

Gran still drives, though she had to take a driving test this year in order to keep her licence. She passed with flying colors.

"Where're we going?"

"You mind goin' to the mall with your old granny? I know how you hate shopping with your mom. I promise I won't make you try on ugly clothes," she says with a giggle. "I need an outfit for my ballroom dancing recital this afternoon."

My mind boggles. I knew Gran took some kind of dance lesson on Sunday afternoons. She heads straight over to the community center after my visits. But ballroom dancing? I thought it was exercise dancing for old folks. Then again, she does go on and on about *Dancing with the Stars*, and how much she loves some guy on the show named Maks, so it shouldn't surprise me. She even painted a picture of him, if I remember correctly.

"How come you never told me you were taking ballroom dancing?"

"Oh, I suppose I do lots of things I don't tell you about," she says with a wink. "Tonight we do the Cha Cha Cha. I'm so excited. I've got to get something sexy, but age appropriate."

She threw in the last bit for my benefit. Gran isn't like Mom in the way she dresses. She's got class. I wish some of it had rubbed off on my mother.

After pulling into the parking lot of Bridgewood Mall in Gran's cherry red 1989 Toyota Corolla SR5, we head into the mall to her favorite dancewear store "Step-in-Style."

"I've got some exciting news," I announce.

"What's that, honey?" she asks as she searches the racks in the Latin dance section.

"I've got a date tonight."

Gran stops, smiles hugely and pulls me into an embrace. "Oh, Lola, I'm so happy for you." Then she holds me at arm's length. "Is he a good boy? What's his name?"

"His name's Jon, and yes, Gran, he's a good boy."

She eyes me for a moment, a brow lifts and her lips purse. "You didn't tell him about The Vanishing did you?"

I chew my lower lip and worry creases my brow as I give a slow nod. Lying to Gran is not an option. But I didn't think she'd ask this question. How stupid am I?

"Oh, Lola." A frown sets on her lips and her face erupts in a road map of wrinkles. "Honey, you've got to be careful who you tell. You told me the other day Charlie knows, but no one else, okay? Only those closest to you should know."

A flicker of regret passes through me. "I... I'm sorry." My gaze falls away.

She takes my hand and pats it. "It's all right, just don't tell anyone else, okay?"

I nod. I'm relieved she's not mad. Upsetting Gran is the last thing I'd ever want to do. "So, who did you tell besides me? Do Mom, Dad and Eva know?" I ask, figuring I should know whether to keep my mouth shut around my family – not that I'd tell them anyway.

Gran gives her head a solemn shake. "No. Your mom and Eva don't have the ability, so there was no sense in telling them. And your dad, well it's none of his business and besides he wouldn't believe it, so why saddle his tiny brain with the knowledge."

Despite Dad saying he loved Gran this morning, I know there's no love lost between them, although I never understood why and never asked. Some things a person's better off not knowing.

"I'm pretty sure I can trust Jon and I *know* I can trust Charlie," I say, trying to look confident. "I haven't told anyone else."

Gran cups my face in her hands. "It's my fault. I should have told you to keep everything quiet last week when we first talked about The Vanishing." She cocks her head and makes a *tsk* sound. "This is all so new to you. I should have taken more time to explain. But, what's done is done and there's no use worrying about it now. Besides, I'm sure your boy's a good fella and I know Charlie's a true friend." She smiles, throws her hands in the air then resumes her search for an age appropriate Cha Cha Cha costume.

The saleswoman appears and helps Gran find the perfect ensemble with matching shoes. It's a tasteful dark blue dress with a slit up one side, but not as high as most of the others. The shoes are navy leather with a sturdy one-inch heel. It's the first and only dress Gran tries on.

"I love it," she declares and, before I know it, we're done.

Shopping with Gran is a whole lot simpler than with Mom.

"Do ya want something new to wear for your date tonight?" Gran asks with excitement in her voice. "I'll treat ya."

"No, it's okay. I've already picked out something to wear." Gran's always trying to give me things or buy me stuff.

"Ah come on, lemme do something nice for my darling granddaughter." She pulls me into the first store she spies that looks like it's for teenagers.

I relent, knowing it's a losing battle anyway and pick out a couple of tops. Not T-shirts, but real tops with buttons. I'd never really considered anything like this for myself before. Suddenly they seem pretty.

"Do ya want to try them on?"

"They're an extra-large, they'll fit," I say flatly, holding one up against me.

Gran pays and I take the bag. I'm already carrying her bags from "Step-in-Style."

"I'm starvin'," Gran says. "Let's go to the food court."

"It's only 11:00," I say, but realize Gran probably didn't have breakfast. "On second thought, I'd love a tea and a muffin."

Grandma Rose sits in front of me with a heaped Styrofoam plate of Chinese food. I've already started in on my blueberry muffin.

"How's your story comin'?"

I tell Gran about everything I write. She's my biggest fan and greatest supporter. "I'm having a bit of trouble with it. But it'll work itself out."

"Good attitude. I know it'll be fantastic when you get done with it. You're going to be a best-selling author someday."

Hearing those words, I feel my heart doing a little dance. It's what I want more than anything. "Do you really think so?"

"I've read everything you're ever written and I'm not just saying it 'cause I love you. You've got talent! Don't you dare let it go to waste. You better let me read this one as soon as you're done." She narrows her eyes in mock threat.

"Don't worry; you'll be the first person I let read it."

"How 'bout your parents? Are they warming up to the idea of you wanting to be a writer?"

I shake my head and think about what my parents want for me. They'd probably be fine with me having a regular-type 9 to 5 job, working in an office somewhere, but they'd never support my dream of being a writer. It's too foreign to them.

Gran shovels in a huge forkful of moo guy chicken and continues to speak despite her full mouth. "You've got to do what you love."

Her words are garbled, but I understand her perfectly.

"Don't be what your parents want you to be. Follow your dreams, Lola. Now's the time – when you're young."

"I know, Gran. I've also got to decide on a major."

"You didn't pick one yet?" Concern tinges her voice. "I think that's a no-brainer … English literature."

She's right. It's what my heart wants, but it's not what's expected of me. "How do I tell Mom and Dad? I feel like I owe them, they're paying my tuition."

"Honey, they're your parents, what do you think they're going to do? Keep you from going to university just because they don't like your major? Besides, whadda they know about university, neither of them dodo birds finished high school."

We laugh until we cry. It's so wonderful to have Gran on my side. It's as if we're the same soul living in separate bodies.

Gran throws a hand in the air, a finger extended. "I've got an idea," she says, her eyes bright.

I lean forward. "Lay it on me."

"A tattoo," she says.

"What?"

"You need to get a tattoo. Nothing too big, mind you. I don't really like tattoos, but this would be a symbol, something to remind you of your passion and your dream of becoming a writer. Like a book, or a pen or even a typewriter."

I shake my head. "That's crazy."

"No, it's not. You can have it put in a place where you'll always see it. It can be a constant reminder to never give up on your dream."

The idea rolls around in my mind for a moment. If it were coming from anyone other than Gran, I'd reject it without a thought, but she does have a good point, and it wouldn't have to be big, just something small, maybe on the inside of my wrist where I'd see it every day.

"There's a tattoo parlour in the mall. Ya wanna do it?" Mischief plays in her eyes.

"My parents would freak. Especially Dad – you know how old fashioned he can be when it comes to his girls."

Gran gives a throaty laugh. "Good Lord. He doesn't have a leg to stand on with all those damn tattoos he's got. Besides, Eva's got one, hasn't she?"

"Yeah, but he didn't like it. She was grounded for two weeks. Besides, she's over eighteen. Don't you have to be eighteen?"

"I'll tell them you're my granddaughter and it's my present to you for your eighteenth birthday. And don't worry about your parents, they'll get over it." Gran's eyes flash with excitement. "If all else fails, I'll give them a little extra dough." She winks.

Excitement is starting to build and I let myself believe it's possible. "I think I'd rather have a capital letter A, you know how they do letters in fancy script? The A would stand for 'author'."

"That sounds like a fine idea." She leans closer and whispers, "So, do ya wanna?"

A part of me wants to say yes, but I think about my date tonight. Getting a tattoo just might get me grounded.

"It's a great idea, but let's do it the next time we're here."

Gran digs into her purse and pulls out her wallet. She holds a clenched fist out over my hand. "Take this and next time you're here, do it."

She stuffs a wad of rolled up bills into my palm.

"There's a little extra in case you need to bribe 'em," she says with a giggle.

"I can't take your money, Gran…"

"Why the hell not? Who else am I gonna give it to? It makes me happy so see you happy. Go ahead, take it. Make an old lady happy."

Seeing how much it means to her to do this for me, I take the money. "Thanks. I promise I'll do it."

Gran scoffs down the rest of her lunch in record time, even before I finish my tea.

"We'd better get back. I've got to get ready for my Cha Cha Cha class and you've got a date."

Chapter Sixteen

I eat my beef stir-fry with enthusiasm. I'm actually enjoying my dinner tonight because it's a nice change from the chicken stir-fry Mom makes at least three times a week.

"Thanks, Mom," I say, rising.

"Not so fast," Dad commands from his post at the head of the table. "You and Eva have to help your mother with the dishes."

Eva sighs.

My lips twist into a snarl and I want to say to Dad, "Why don't *you* ever have to help Mom with the dishes?" but instead I move at top speed, clearing, scraping and rinsing, finally piling all the dishes into the dishwasher. Eva and Mom watch wide-eyed and no doubt delighted by the one-woman show.

"Okay? Can I go now?"

Dad nods and I make my escape only to freeze when I hear Eva speak.

"Lola has a date," she announces loud enough for me to hear from the hallway. I try to creep away on tiptoes to the safety of my room.

"Lola!" Dad calls. "Get back here!"

Shit, shit, shit.

I slink back into the kitchen, cringing.

Despite his funky appearance, Dad's old fashioned. He points to my chair. "Sit down."

I sit.

"Is it true?" he asks. "You have a date?"

"With a boy?" Mom adds.

My gaze drops to the floor and I steel myself for their reaction. "Yes," I whisper.

Then the unthinkable happens. They laugh, but in a good way. Dad's hands come together in a big clap and Mom's bouncing with joy. I look up, unbelieving.

Eva sits sour-faced and disappointed.

"Finally," Dad says, smiling.

"So, what's his name?" Mom asks. "How old is he?" Her voice drips with gratitude and relief.

"He's a senior like me. His name's Jon."

"Is he Italian?" Dad asks with genuine excitement on his face.

"No, Dad, he's not Italian," I say flatly. For some reason, Dad's got it in his head that if you're not Italian, then you're just not as good. Don't know why he married a woman of Irish descent.

Dad's shoulders deflate. "Oh well, not everyone can be Italian."

"Where's he taking you?" Mom is on her feet and standing behind me, fluffing my hair. "Can I help you get ready?"

"Ah, no thanks. I've got it covered." I try to look grateful. "And we're meeting at the movie theater."

"Well then, get going, don't keep the boy waiting," Dad says and I'm gone before another thought can hit their heads.

The fact Dad doesn't seem to mind that Jon's not coming to the front door to pick me up like boys did in the old days, shocks me, but I guess he's just relieved I have a date, and that I'm not a lesbian.

I shower and shampoo my mop of dark curls. The way I wear my hair's never really been a concern before, but tonight I pull out Eva's assortment of brushes and hair products. After spritzing on something that claims it will make my hair shine, and rubbing in a palmful of mousse, I blow dry my hair with the aid of a big round brush. I yank and pull until my curls are now shiny, straight locks. Then I use Eva's flat iron to straighten it further and get rid of any leftover frizz.

"Shit," I mutter when the iron touches my forehead, leaving a tiny puckered burn. Thankfully, it's close enough to my hairline; I don't think anyone will notice.

I make a mental note – be careful of straightening irons in the future. They're pretty damn hot!

Once back in my room, I slide my iPod into its speaker base and crank the tunes while surveying myself in the dresser mirror. *Not bad.* My hair is shiny and very, very straight. It's a nice change.

Since this is all new to me, I don't know whether to dress first or put on my make-up. I decide on the make-up and take out my tiny zippered pouch. It contains a black eye-liner, mascara and two light pink lip glosses. Not much of a selection.

I creak open my door and look across the hall to Eva's room. *Should I chance it or not?* Eva's got enough make-up to stock a cosmetics store. I cock my head and listen. There's still conversation and noise coming from the kitchen. I tiptoe across the hall. Eva's coming up the stairs. *Ah hell*, it's like she's got some kind of radar or something.

"What are you doing, freak?"

"Nothing," I say and slam my door.

A moment later, there's a knock and Eva pushes my door open. "Thought you might want to borrow this," she says and walks in with what I can only describe as a suitcase of make-up.

She hefts it onto my desk and after flicking about a half a dozen latches open, she unfolds tray upon tray of lipsticks and glosses, mascaras and colored liners, shadows and bronzers. There are brushes of every size, tweezers and lash curlers. In the very bottom, every color of nail polish imaginable shines up at me.

"No way! You're going to let me borrow your make-up?"

Eva flips her hair over a shoulder and chews on her lip, and for a second I'm afraid she's going to pack up and leave.

"Why not?" she says finally. "You need all the help you can get. Just don't mess it up. Put everything back in

76

its place, then close it up and put it back in my closet. Okay?"

She makes me feel like a five-year-old, but I nod with hearty enthusiasm.

Eva smirks and leaves me alone with her treasure trove. Her gesture means a lot because I know how much the suitcase of make-up means to her. She lugs it to and from beauty school every day. It's her life and will one day be the source of her livelihood.

"Thank you," I call after her but I'm met with the slam of a door; though the slam was less emphatic than usual.

After perusing the cornucopia of beauty products before me, I choose a purple eye-liner and shimmering beige shadow to match my new top. I curl my lashes, apply mascara and pink lip gloss, then take a look in the mirror on the inside lid of the case. A smile stretches across my face. I look pretty damn cute, if I do say so myself.

In about half an hour I've got to meet Jon at the theater. I decide to ask for a drive over there so I won't have to walk. Suddenly I'm afraid my hair will get blown around – that's a new thought for me. God, I'm turning into such a girl.

Earrings are in; one more look in the mirror and I'm good to go.

The phone rings as I head downstairs. I'm thankful for the distraction, since Mom's the one who answered. She won't be able to make a fuss now.

"No!" Mom shrieks. "Is she okay?"

I listen for a moment at the bottom of the stairs. The concern in her voice has me rooted to the spot.

"We're on our way."

And just like that, my life's flipped upside down.

Chapter Seventeen

"No!" I scream when Mom tells me.

Gran collapsed during her Cha Cha Cha. It was a heart attack. My world stops and a fear, huge and black, looms, threatening to devour me. I want to run, scream, and hit something. I want to curse at God for being so cruel, but I can't add to my parent's distress. Everyone's at the front door, pulling on sweaters and shoes and gathering purses, wallets and car keys. My heart flutters, but I will myself to stay visible by taking long, slow deep breaths. The Vanishing can't take me now even though I wish it would.

"Lola, let's go!" Dad yells.

I'm frozen, immobile with dread at the thought of what state I'll find Grandma Rose in at the hospital. *Please God, don't take her away from me.* My prayers are to the same God I hated only moments before.

"Which hospital did you say?" Dad asks when we get into the car.

"St. Joseph's," Mom answers. I think without comfort, *it's the same hospital where I was born.*

The drive to the hospital is eerily silent. The only sound is Mom's occasional muttering into the air around her, "Please God, don't let her die."

My fear has vanished and is replaced with numbness and disbelief as we walk through the sliding doors of St. Joseph's. An elderly man sitting at a reception desk tells us where we can find Gran. She's in Intensive Care and only one of us can go in at a time.

Dad, Eva and I sit on plastic upholstered green chairs in the waiting room. All around us are tear-stained faces, hands grasping balled-up tissues and a few people pacing laps around the room. I fight the urge to scream at the pacers to stop. My own nervous energy is ready to explode.

Eva and Dad haven't shed a tear. Eva is disobeying the "no cellphones" rule which is printed on a large yellow placard above her head. Her fingers move with practised precision as she texts her friends. No doubt this drama is providing her with some extra attention. I want to rip the phone from her hand, stomp on it and kick the shit out of her.

The thought flashes briefly through my mind: I've now officially stood Jon up. It's not a priority now, only Gran is. Minutes pass like hours and, finally, Mom walks through the doors that have "Intensive Care Unit. Only one visitor per person" written across them in bold, black lettering.

Mascara-streaked tears run down her cheeks, making her look ridiculous and pitiful at the same time, and suddenly I realize I must look the same. But I don't care.

"How is she?" I say, jumping to my feet.

Mom shakes her head. "Not good."

This isn't real. This can't be happening. I want to feel sad, but the tears that came so easily earlier refuse to come now. A tremor of anger runs through me. How unfair it all seems.

"She wants you," Mom says, looking at me.

Eva gazes up from her phone. "What about me?"

Mom sits in my chair and plants her head on Dad's shoulder. She presses a wadded-up tissue to her eyes.

"What about me?" Eva asks again as I walk on elastic legs toward the ominous doors.

The doors are locked. Confused, I look around until I spy the sign instructing visitors to push a buzzer. I will my fingers to the tiny white button and press. There's a click and I push the doors open. I'm met on the other side by a nurse sitting at a desk.

"Who are you visiting?" she asks in a serious whisper.

"Rose Powers," I say, but I already see Gran in the bed farthest from the door.

I walk toward her as the nurse says, "Bed 8."

The room is large and dimly lit. Most of the beds are encircled by a curtain. Sobs and groans and the beeping of machines emanate from behind them. The numbness and shock begins to fall away and the hot sting of tears prick my eyes.

"Gran?" I whisper as I approach. She's not lying flat. Her bed is on an angle. Wires run from her chest under her hospital gown to a monitor that beeps along with her heart. An I.V. drips a clear liquid slowly into her veins and an oxygen mask covers her small face.

"Kiddo," she says in a papery thin voice. Her lips are dry and cracked but she manages a small smile.

"I love you," I say and start to cry.

She reaches a shaky hand for me.

I take it and cover it in kisses. "I love you so much," I choke out between sobs.

"I love you too," she says slowly and her own tears fall.

I pull a hard plastic chair as close as I can to the bed and sit, all the while holding Gran's hand. The skin is thin, almost transparent and gray. The blue of her veins is vivid beneath it. I want to crawl into bed with her and hug her to me, but settle for stroking her cheek.

"You have to get better." I give a little smile. "I can't live without you."

"Yes, you can," Gran replies and nudges the oxygen mask from her face.

"But I don't want to."

I finger-comb her hair which has been flattened by her pillow. It's finer than I thought and I can see her scalp. "You should put the mask back on."

She shakes her head. "Too hard to talk."

I sneak a peek at the nurse who's not looking our way. "I guess it's okay, for a little while."

Gran signals for me to come closer and I lean in a little more.

"I need to tell you something." Her voice is barely a whisper.

"You should save your strength. We can talk tomorrow." I dab away her tears with a tissue.

With a slow shake of her head, she meekly pulls me closer still.

"What is it?" I ask, seeing the urgency in her eyes.

"It's not menopause."

For a second I think she's not quite right in her head and a tinge of fear jolts me.

"The Vanishing," she says with more vigor, and I suddenly understand.

"It won't go away with menopause?"

"No," she answers. "It will stop when you're ready to be *seen*."

I take a breath and puzzle over this. "I don't understand."

"When. You. Love. Yourself." She pronounces each word slowly and distinctly.

"I'll stop vanishing when I love myself?"

Gran nods and smiles. "Yes."

"Why didn't you tell me this before?"

"I wanted you to find out for yourself." A little light shines in her eyes. "It would mean more."

Strangely, I want to laugh and have to swallow the urge, but I can see the laughter in Gran's eyes. She was forever telling me that once a woman gets through menopause, she won't care what the world thinks of her any more.

I'm torn. Dealing with my ability has been stressful, but at times it's been... useful. I quickly weigh the pros and cons and decide I'd be happier if I were just normal. No more disappearing – good-bye to The Vanishing.

"Then that's what I'm going to do, Gran. As soon as you get out of the hospital, you can help me."

"I won't always be around, Lola honey." The beeps on the monitor suddenly grow in intensity then calm again. Gran's eyes are focused on me. She's staring, as if savoring this moment; as if she thinks it'll be our last.

From the corner of my eye, I catch sight of the nurse heading our way.

"Time's just about up, young lady. Your grandma needs her rest."

"Please, just another minute," I say and Gran's grip tightens in agreement.

"One more minute," she says, slipping the mask back over Gran's nose and mouth. Then she treads silently back to her post.

My eyes reconnect with Gran's.

"I have to go now, Grandma. I love you with all my heart and when I come to see you tomorrow, I know you'll be better." I force a smile and kiss her forehead.

I walk backwards waving and smiling through my tears. Grandma Rose grows smaller and smaller as I walk past the nurse and stand at the door for one last look. She's so frail and ancient looking.

She blows me a kiss.

Chapter Eighteen

On the way home, I borrow Eva's cellphone and text Charlie. I tell her about Gran and can barely see through my tear-filled eyes. I don't have Jon's cell number and though my mind is on Gran, I can't help but feel bad for standing him up. Charlie offers to go to the movie theater to see if he's still there, but I tell her not to worry about it. I'll explain everything when I see him. Besides, there's no way he's still there. We were supposed to meet hours ago.

Eva eyes me, bouncing a leg impatiently.

"Thanks." I hand back the phone.

She grunts something unintelligible and immediately her fingers begin to fly again. Eva hasn't lost a beat, despite the tragedy now hovering, watching with hooded eyes, for its opportunity to pounce.

"Do you think Grandma Rose will be okay?" I ask Mom.

She sniffs back tears and turns around in her seat to face me. "The doctor said the next twenty-four hours are the most crucial. If she has a good night, she may pull through."

May pull through? I push those negative words from my mind. Denial is my friend right now.

"Maybe someone should have stayed with her," I say, alarmed at the thought of Gran being alone. "Maybe she's scared."

"There's nothing we can do for her right now, honey," Dad says. "She needs her rest more than anything else and I'm sure they're making her comfortable."

"I'm not going to school tomorrow. I want to stay with Gran at the hospital," I state in a tone that says I mean business.

"No, you have to go to school," Mom replies, trumping me. "We'll go straight to the hospital as soon as you get home."

"She can't be alone."

"Dad and I will stay with her. We'll stay at the hospital all day, but probably won't get to see her much until she's out of Intensive Care and in her own room."

"When will that be?"

"I don't know, honey." Mom's eyes dart briefly to Dad, who returns the look with a sidelong glance.

There's something ominous and not quite right about that look, it's as if they have a secret they don't want to share. My stomach clenches and suddenly it's hard to breathe. The confines of the car feel as if they're closing in around me. With frantic urgency, I roll down my window and stick my head out; drawing in cool lungful's of air. The world isn't the same. I can't stand this horrible feeling, like there's a part of me missing. Gran may recover. But she's eighty; how many more years could I possibly have with her?

It's dark when we get home and the night suffocates me. I run into the house, needing the safety of my room. The cool of the windowpane feels good on my forehead as I stare out into the still of the evening. Suddenly, it's as if a wet blanket has been thrown over me, and my heart beats in uncontrollable flip-flops, stealing my breath.

Undiluted terror begins to rise from my feet until a wave of panic overtakes me. I'm going to die. I'm sure of it. My heart bangs so hard, sharp pains stab the left side of my chest. I pace, trying to quell my terror, but it's no use. Despair has taken me in rough hands. It's as if I'm watching myself from outside of my body, as I run downstairs to my parents. I can't breathe. My legs barely carry me as I stumble into the room.

Mom's curled up on the couch, still sniffling and dabbing wet eyes. She's on the phone. Dad's lying in his chair, feet up, head back and eyes closed. The everyday "normal" sounds of the television are disorienting and offensive, and I desperately want it turned off. Nothing is normal or okay. The world is a horrible, terrifying place. How can anyone be happy when unspeakable things happen to the people we love?

"Mom, I don't feel right." I pace and pull at my collar. My throat is tight. I'm choking.

"Mom?"

She ignores me.

"Dad?" I almost scream. His eyes remain closed.

I run to the sliding patio door and try to open it, but my hand passes through the handle. "Shit," I mutter, realizing I've vanished. Again I try. Despite my panic, I focus on the door handle, and by sheer force of will, this time I feel it solid and cool in my hand. With a yank, it opens and I step out into the late spring evening, inhaling until my heart slows. It's nice to be free of the house; to be outside in what passes for nature in suburbia.

I turn to see Mom and Dad staring at me wide-eyed and slack-jawed.

"That door opened by itself," Mom says, the phone still clenched in her hand now hangs by her side.

"How did you…?" Dad's words trail off and he runs a hand through his spiky hair.

"I was here the whole time. You just didn't notice me," I say quickly. "I didn't feel well. I couldn't breathe and it felt like my throat was closing up on me. I needed air."

They nod in unison. How else could they react? They've just witnessed the impossible.

"I'm gonna try to get some sleep." I turn to leave.

"Do you want to talk?" Mom asks, following me up the stairs to my room.

I feel a bit better now, but a part of me still wants my mother. "Sure," I say, grateful for the offer.

Mom settles on the bed beside me. "You probably had an anxiety attack because of how scared you are for Grandma Rose."

"Anxiety attack?" I've heard the words before but can't fathom actually being attacked by anxiety.

"It's when you feel panicky and your heart beats too fast and you can't breathe. I've had them, so I know how you must have felt. They're absolutely horrible." She rests a hand on my knee. "Are you okay now?"

Anxiety attack. I mull it over. It makes sense. Worry again floods my mind. "What if it comes back? What if Gran dies?" My hands curl into fists and my shoulders hunch to my ears.

"Lola, you need to calm down." Mom takes my hands and smoothes them open. "Why don't you lie down and do some deep breathing. Try not to think worried thoughts."

"Okay," I croak, and slide my bulk down until my head hits the pillow. My breathing is shallow at first, but as Mom runs a hand over my hair and caresses my cheek, it soon falls into a slow, steady rhythm.

"Things have a way of working themselves out, honey. If the worst happens, you will get over it, in time. Think of how bad I felt when Grandpa Ken died. You were just little and didn't understand what was going on at the time, but I lost my father, who I loved very much and yet, life went on for me."

"It hurts so bad right now. How much worse can it get?" Tears run down my cheeks and are absorbed by my pillow.

Mom grabs some tissue from my night table and wipes my face. "I'm still here and I'm not going anywhere for a very long time. You still have me." She leans over and kisses my cheek.

I sigh. How can I tell her I prefer Gran over her? That maybe I love Gran more?

"I know, Mom, thanks."

"You looked beautiful tonight. I'm sorry I didn't get a chance to tell you. I'm sorry your night was ruined."

My stomach knots at the thought of Jon and of what could have been. "Nothing matters more than Grandma Rose getting better. It's okay."

"This too shall pass."

More tears come with those words. Gran always says the same thing.

Mom wipes away her own tears. "I hate to see you in so much pain."

"I'll be okay." My eyes are heavy and burn from crying. "I just want to sleep now," I tell her, needing to be alone with my thoughts.

She gets up and stands by my door, looking haggard and worn; tiny and frail. Her eyes glisten wetly. "Do you want me to turn off your light?"

"Yes."

I'm left with the soft glow of the nightlight I still haven't outgrown, as the door clicks shut behind her. I open my night table drawer and pull out the blankie I haven't needed for years. Grandma Rose knitted it when I was a baby. Its fuzzy softness brings back memories of childhood. I inhale its familiar scent and calm settles over me, enough at least to take me to sleep's antechamber.

My sleep is thin and filled with anxiety-riddled nightmares. In my dreams, Grandma Rose is hit by a bus and tossed broken and bleeding to the side of the road. Unable to get to her, I can only watch helplessly as she dies. There's some sort of invisible barrier that I'm not allowed to cross. A jolt of adrenaline propels me awake and I sit straight up. I glance at the glowing red numbers of my alarm clock – 5:30.

It takes a moment until I remember Gran's heart attack. Grayness descends, settling heavy on my chest and I will myself out of bed. My room is suffocatingly small and

I need to get out. I go downstairs still dressed in yesterday's clothes.

Mom is nursing a coffee in the living room and turns to me as I enter.

"Have you phoned the hospital yet?" I ask.

"Yes, they said she had a restless night but she's resting comfortably now."

I settle beside her. She looks older, like she's aged ten years in one night and I realize that I'm not the only one hurting. Grandma Rose is my grandmother, but she's also Mom's mother. I hold out my arms and pull my mother into an embrace. It feels odd, yet wonderful and I wonder why we don't do this very much. Guilt creeps over me; guilt at being so selfish. Maybe Mom needed me last night and I let her in just enough, until I felt better and then pushed her away.

Her shoulders heave. She's crying.

"This too shall pass," I whisper and she hugs me tighter.

Chapter Nineteen

Despite one last attempt at convincing my parents to let me go to the hospital with them, Dad forced me to go to school.

Charlie was waiting at my locker. She wanted to walk to school with me, but I needed some time to myself, to think.

"Sorry about Gran," she says, giving me a sympathetic pout.

I sniff and pinch away the tears blurring my vision. "She's going to pull through. She's a fighter."

"Is that what the doctor said?" A ghost of a smile shadows her lips.

"No, it's what *I* say."

Her smile fades. "Oh," she whispers and drops her gaze.

"I vanished last night," I say quietly, suddenly sorry for my harsh tone.

"Oh, no. Where?" Charlie's eyes widen with alarm. "Not at the hospital?"

"No, at home. My parents kinda noticed. But I made up a good cover story and I think they bought it."

"Phew. What happened?"

"I was having a hard time dealing with Gran being in the hospital and all, so I ran to my parents for help. It was so weird. It was like my throat was closing up and I couldn't breathe. They were in the living room and when I walked in, at first I thought they were ignoring me. Then I realized I must be invisible." My hand flutters to my throat and I pull on the collar of my T-shirt. "But something interesting happened this time."

Charlie crowds closer. "What?"

"I found a way to move things. I opened the patio door. First my hand went right through the handle, but when I really, really concentrated, I did it."

She gasps and grabs my hands. "Do you know what this means?"

"I know. It was the one flaw in our plan."

A broad grin expands across her face, but is quickly replaced by a more solemn expression, as if she'd just realized she should match my mood out of some unwritten rule from the best friend code of conduct.

"Sorry. We can talk about this another time. I know you've got a lot on your mind right now."

She holds her arms out for a hug and I bend to meet her embrace. "It's okay, Char, really."

"We've got to get to class anyway. Just know I'm thinking of you and I'll be saying prayers for Gran."

The genuine concern in her voice coaxes more tears. I quickly wipe them away. "Thanks," I whisper, but I want to say more. I want to tell her how much I love her and how thankful I am to have her as my friend. But she breaks the embrace and the moment has passed. We part ways and head to our respective homerooms.

Jon's not in class yet when I slide into my usual seat. The morning announcements start and soon after we're standing for the national anthem. Still no Jon. My eyes keep darting to the door, hoping he's just late. I desperately want a chance to explain what happened last night. To watch his eyes as I tell him, so I can make sure he still likes me. As Gran always says, "The eyes are the windows of the soul."

Halfway through class, I give up my search and turn to stare out the window. The sky is blue and cloudless and the grass freshly mowed. Wild flowers bloom at the edges of the groomed field. I marvel at how life goes on, how the sun still shines and people smile and laugh, while my heart slowly crumbles.

Class is over and my ears prick up when I hear my name over the PA. "Lola Savullo to the office, please." Panic swells my throat and an icy-fingered tendril of dread slides slowly down my spine. Being called to the office can only mean bad news.

I make it out of the classroom on rubber legs before the fog rolls in and I begin to fall, seemingly in slow motion, caving in on myself like a tent without poles. Someone's caught my arm. There's a call for help, but it sounds so far away.

When I open my eyes, there's a crowd. I'm lying on my back on the cold, hard floor of the corridor. Someone's book bag is tucked under my head: a makeshift pillow.

Mrs. Wright kneels by my side, and gently slaps my face while calling my name.

"I fainted," I say, more of a declaration than a question.

"Yes," she replies. Concern looms in her expression.

With noodle arms I try to push myself up off the floor.

"Whoa, let's wait for Mrs. Dalhiwal." She places a gentle hand on my shoulder in an effort to keep me in place until the school nurse arrives.

"Okay, everyone, she's all right," Mrs. Wright announces to my audience. "You can all go to class now."

The crowd slowly disperses. There are whispers and lingering glances.

A deep, rolling groan escapes me when I see my father running toward us. I'm vaguely aware of the accented voice of the school nurse, asking me how I feel. I push her away and stagger to my feet. She huffs her displeasure. "Please, young lady. Let me check if you are all right. Do not be moving around yet."

I move past her and into Dad's arms.

"Did she...?" I whisper.

"Yes," he replies.

Chapter Twenty

"We have to go to the hospital. Mom and Eva are already there," Dad whispers into my hair.

Mrs. Dalhiwal and Mrs. Wright linger for a while, but soon walk away, leaving me and Dad in privacy.

The bell for second period rings and the halls are now finally empty.

"No. I can't."

Dad holds me at arm's length. "Lola, don't you want to say good-bye before they take her to..."

I hold out a hand and turn away. "No, don't say it." I can't let my mind wander to the funeral home and what they'll do to my poor Gran. "There's no one to say good-bye to now, Dad. Grandma Rose is gone." My composure surprises me.

"But your mother will want you with her at a time like this."

"She'll have you and Eva. Please, there's something really important I have to do. I'll see you at home tonight."

He opens his mouth to speak and I expect a fight, but his expression softens and he lets out a sigh. "All right. Whatever it is you need to do; I can tell it's important to you. I trust you, Lola."

"Thanks." I kiss his stubbly cheek and run down the hallway and out the rear doors, before he can change his mind.

My textbooks are still scattered on the hall floor. I suppose Dad will pick them up. I can't make myself care about anything except the mission I'm now on. My small purse is still slung across my shoulders and I'm grateful I didn't lose it when I fainted, or that no one took it from around my neck to make me more comfortable.

My legs throb and my chest feels like it's going to explode by the time I make it to the road and climb aboard the 64B westbound.

The same sense of disbelief I felt the day before settles over me as I sit in shocked silence. The bumpy bus ride lulls me into a place of comfort. Maybe I should have asked Charlie to come with me, I think, but know deep down this is something I have to do on my own.

After twenty minutes, the bus pulls into the parking lot of the Bridgewood Mall and I get off, sleepy and strangely calm. I pretend Gran's with me and even speak out loud as if she's at my side. A few sidelong glances are thrown my way by passers-by, but it doesn't matter. The sense of Gran's presence gives me strength.

Up ahead, the silver and navy U-Nique Tattoos and Piercings sign looms. Before today, I would have been nervous to go in, but right now, in this very moment, I'm more than ready.

I'm greeted by a skinny blond man with pin straight shoulder-length hair only a woman should be allowed to have. He's wearing a white wife-beater, no doubt to show off his two full sleeves of tattoos. He's a younger version of Brett Michaels. But instead of a bandana, he's wearing a black leather cowboy hat.

"I know I should have an appointment," I say, "but this is kind of an emergency."

He throws his head back and laughs. "That's the first time I've heard that." He's tall and blue-eyed and really cute.

"I need a tattoo. Can you do it?"

"Of course. It's perfect timing. Nobody's here." He makes a sweeping gesture around the room. "First, I'm gonna need picture ID. You have to be eighteen or have written parental consent if you're under the age of majority." He speaks as if he's memorized a script.

I throw my shoulders back and hold my head high as I reach into my purse. "My grandmother is treating me to a tattoo for my eighteenth birthday. I want a very small two-color one on my wrist. I'm sorry I don't have ID on me, but I do have this." I hold out the wad of bills Gran gave me just days ago.

He eyes the money greedily.

"There's two hundred and fifty dollars here. I wouldn't think a tattoo the size I want would cost more than a hundred."

His blue eyes dart from side-to-side. He snatches the bills and quickly pockets them. "Okay, come on. But if your parents get mad and come down here, I'm denying everything. Got that?" He looks concerned, but his voice is grinning.

"My parents are probably your best customers," I say matter-of-factly.

A smile sweeps across his face. "Is that right? Well then, I guess they won't mind that you're following the family tradition." He ushers me to the back of the store.

The walls are lined with picture after picture of scary looking people with tattoos and piercings. Charlie would be more comfortable here than I am. There are no other customers but there is a burly dude reading what looks like a magazine on tattoos.

"That's Billy, he's my business partner."

Billy doesn't look up, only offers a grunt as we pass.

"Name's Ben, by the way."

"Lola."

"Pleasure to meet you, Lola. Sounds like you've got a pretty liberal family."

I smile and nod. *You don't know the half of it.*

"On your wrist you say?"

"Yes, very small on the inside of my left wrist. About this big." I hold up my forefinger and thumb an inch apart.

"No prob. A tatt that size won't take long at all."

We enter a small room and Ben closes the door behind us. There's a cushioned table in the center, like

94

you'd find in a doctor's office. One wall is painted bright red and the others are yellow. Black lacquered shelves hold various knick-knacks, many of which are figurines of skulls of various shapes and sizes.

"Hop on." Ben pats the table.

I slide my butt onto it, swing my legs up and lie back.

He's holding a photo album. "Do you already know what you want or do you wanna look at our tattoo gallery?"

"I know exactly what I want."

Chapter Twenty-One

Thankfully, I'm home before the rest of my family and have time to change into a long sleeved top. Ben wrapped my tender left wrist in gauze, which I am to keep on overnight. He gave me a small tube of antibacterial cream to rub on every day for a week and instructed me not to get my "fresh ink" wet. Although I feel kinda cool and can't wait to show it off to Charlie, I think this one tiny tattoo will be my first and last work of body art.

It's the last gift I will ever receive from Grandma Rose and it comforts me to know it'll last a lifetime. I smile. "Thanks Gran," I say to the air around me. "You will always be a part of my life. I will never forget you and I'll always love you."

I text Charlie and tell her about Grandma Rose and my tattoo. She'd already heard I'd fainted after first period and figured it must have been because of something bad. Apparently, I was the talk of the school for the entire afternoon.

Even though I knew she'd be trying to reach me, I'd needed to be out of touch for a while and had turned off my phone. Worrying Charlie was not what I'd intended, and thankfully, she understood. She offers to come over, but I tell her it's probably best if she doesn't since I don't know when my family will be home. Charlie would be uncomfortable in such a highly emotional atmosphere, so sparing her the agony is the least I can do.

I make a cup of tea and this simple act makes tears bloom in my eyes. Will every task, no matter how small, remind me of Grandma Rose for the rest of my life? Will the pain of her loss follow me 'til the day I die?

I curl up on the couch and turn on the TV as a distraction. If only I could turn *off* my mind. Every time I close my eyes, I see her, my beautiful grandmother, lying in that hospital bed, so tiny and pale. The inevitable advice will be that I should be grateful she lived a long life. She went quickly, without much suffering, they'll say, but that's such bullshit. None of that matters. It wouldn't matter if she were a hundred and eighty; I'd miss her because she took with her my sense of safety in this world. Now, all I feel is fear and anxiety at the fragility of life. I miss her so much my heart actually aches.

The low rumble of the garage door opening alerts me to the fact my family is home. A moment later, the door from the garage to the house opens, and soft voices in conversation spill into the room.

"Lola?" Mom calls.

"In here."

She runs to me and holds out her arms. I bend to her embrace and allow myself to be mothered.

"Oh, honey, are you okay? Daddy told me what happened."

Eva walks past with Dad carrying bags into the kitchen. Tears glisten in her usually emotionless eyes.

"I'm fine."

"Where were you?" she asks, breaking our embrace.

"I had something to do. Are *you* okay?"

Mom nods unconvincingly. "We were at the funeral home… making arrangements."

My stomach tightens and bile threatens to rise. I turn away and start for the kitchen.

"Lola." Mom stops me in my tracks. "The wake is tomorrow and the funeral the day after. She wanted to be cremated."

My blood drains to my feet. The idea of Gran being put into the cold, hard ground is bad enough, but the thought of her being burned is just too much. "Thanks for that little tidbit, Mom. I'm not going. I can't, *I won't* see Gran in a coffin." My lips compress into an unyielding line as I watch my mother's expression turn from sad to hurt.

"And how could you let Grandma Rose be burned? It's barbaric."

I leave her and walk into the kitchen where Eva and Dad have spread out Italian take-out on the table.

Eva holds out a plate for me.

"No thanks. Not hungry."

She gives it to Mom who's followed me in. Mom takes it and plunks it down roughly on the counter where its clank grabs our attention. With the kitchen suddenly quiet, she seizes my wrist and turns me roughly to face her. "Don't you…"

My scream stops her. I yank my arm away, my shriek trails into a moan and I cradle my throbbing left wrist against my chest.

Mom jumps. "What's wrong? Did you hurt yourself when you fainted?" She moves in closer for a look. "I'm sorry. I didn't mean to hurt you."

I have an audience of three as Mom gently takes my left hand and pushes up my sleeve.

"It's okay. I'm fine," I reply. I'd been an ass and I know it. "I'm sorry, too. I shouldn't have spoken to you like that."

Dad and Eva look bewildered, having missed the little exchange in the living room, but instead of delving into that minefield, Dad points to my gauze-wrapped wrist and says, "You did hurt yourself. Why didn't you tell us?"

I take a deep trembling breath and hold my head high. "I'm not hurt. I got a tattoo this afternoon."

"What?" Dad almost screams.

Eva smiles. "Lemme see."

"You didn't ask our permission," Mom chimes in. "You're too young for a tattoo."

"Don't be hypocrites," I say with narrowed eyes. "You and Dad are covered in ink. Even Eva has one."

"Two," she corrects.

"Two," I repeat.

My eyes rove from tattoo to tattoo as I eye my mother. There's the flower at the base of her neck, her name in Japanese characters on her own left wrist and the horseshoe on her right ankle, put there for good luck for when she goes to the casino or bingo. And there are more undercover. I'm frequently treated to the huge multi-colored butterfly at the top of her ass crack when she sits in her low-cut jeans; that one's the most cringe-worthy.

"Heidi, she's right. We don't have a leg to stand on here," Dad says, a sheepish grin on his face. "Look at us for Christ's sake. We're her role models. It was bound to happen sooner or later and I suppose she needed something to help her through her grief." He pushes a sleeve up. The familiar colorful sleeve of tats greets me. Despite my bottomless well of embarrassment at dear ole Dad's multitude of tattoos, Dad just wouldn't be Dad without them. And I suppose they make Mom who she is too.

Mom sighs and relents. "Okay, we're all under a lot of stress here." She clears her throat and looks as if she's steeling herself for the unveiling. "Let's see it."

Gingerly, I unwrap the gauze, and as I unroll each layer my heart quickens. I hold out my new body art for all to see.

"A rose," Mom whispers. "It's beautiful."

Chapter Twenty-Two

Dinner is peaceful and even kinda fun. Mom and Dad tell Eva and me the stories behind some of their tattoos. I'd heard a few before, but my interest has blossomed now because I finally feel a part of the in-crowd, a part of my family and all it took was one tiny tattoo. I wonder if Grandma Rose, in all her wisdom, suspected this might happen and I can't help but smile at the thought.

"This one here," Dad says rolling up his pant leg and pointing to a black and white dog on the back of his calf. "This is the first dog I ever owned. She was a Boston Terrier and her name was Lila."

"Lila?" I say. "That's pretty close to my name."

Dad cocks a brow and eyes Mom. "Should we tell her?"

"Why not?" Mom answers with a giggle.

"Well, we named you after the dog," Dad says with a grin and a husky chuckle.

"I didn't really want to," Mom adds quickly, "so we came up with a compromise and changed the 'i' to an 'o'. Besides, Lola's a cool, sexy name."

Yeah, and one that doesn't fit me, I'm tempted to say. I look more like a Jane or an Anne, or some other non-descript blend into the background kind of name.

Eva howls with laughter and bits of chewed food escape before she can clamp a hand over her mouth.

I don't know how to take this bit of news – kinda-sorta named after a dog. Could I really expect anything else from my weirdo parents? Mom and Dad have always marched to the beat of an insane drummer.

"How did Eva get her name?" I ask, hoping for a story more embarrassing than mine.

This brings another conspiratorial look from my parents. Eva sits in rapt attention and I wonder why we've never heard these stories before.

"We really had no idea what to call her," says Mom.

"So we came up with three names and put them in a hat," Dad continues.

"I guess you knew you were having a girl then," I ask.

"No, actually we only had boy names picked because a psychic told us we were going to have a son. We didn't name Eva until she was three days old," Mom explains, "that's why we did the hat thing. We weren't prepared for a girl and had to come up with something fast. Anyway, the three names we decided on were Minerva, after the Roman goddess, Artemis who was a Greek goddess and of course Eva."

"Why Eva?" I ask. "It doesn't go with those other names."

Dad throws his hands in the air. "We just liked it."

"Anyway," Mom continues, "Minerva was the first pick and we actually put it on the birth certificate, but Grandma Rose was fuming mad. She gave us royal hell, saying the poor child would be made fun of her entire life if we gave her that name, so we changed it to Eva."

"You have got to be kidding," says Eva, clearly not amused.

A smile slowly unfurls across my face. The story didn't disappoint. "What's so bad about Minerva?" I can barely keep a straight face. "We could have called you Minnie. Or if they named you Artemis, Artie would have been cute."

"Ha, ha, ha," Eva says with a sneer. I file away this little tidbit to break out as needed at a later date. Being named Minerva, even if it was for a couple of days, is far worse than being named after a dog.

After dinner, we move into the living room and talk about Grandma Rose and the special memories we have of her.

"Gran was my best friend," I say, immediately hating the lame sound of the words as they leave my mouth. She was so much more than that, and there's no way to adequately convey what she meant to me. Words just can't cut it.

Mom smiles, but it's the expression under the expression that tells me I've hurt her. I suppose I said what she'd always suspected. Now she knows I love Gran more than her. Even though regret creeps through me, there's no taking my words back.

She looks away and clears her throat. "Hey, why don't we go upstairs and pick out some pictures from different times in Gran's life," Mom suggests. "I was going to do it later. I figured I wouldn't be able to sleep tonight."

Mom's already neatly swept her hurt feelings under the rug. Might as well carry on as if nothing's wrong. Mom, Eva and me head upstairs to the spare room to go through pictures. I'm surprised Mom has so many photo albums as well as boxes full of pictures.

"Gran gave them to me a couple of months ago." Mom pats one of the old flower-print boxes. "Almost as if she knew something was going to happen."

"Well, she *was* old," Eva says.

I give her a quick slap on the arm.

"Ouch!" She clamps a hand over the red spot I left and steps away.

Mom ignores our bickering and continues, "The funeral home will need them first thing in the morning to make a memory montage. The photos are scanned and then shown on television screens placed throughout the room during the wake."

I pull out a few of Gran and me. In one she's holding me when I was a baby. I know it's me 'cause it's written in faded ink on the back of the picture in Gran's neat script.

"You know, she was the first person to hold you when you were born," Mom says. "Even before your Dad or me." She shakes her head and gives a little laugh. "Gran got right in there and took you out of the nurse's arms. I remember what she said like it was yesterday."

"What'd she say?" I ask.

"She said you were just a peanut of a thing." Mom looks into my eyes. "You only weighed five pounds ten ounces when you were born. You were the tiniest little thing."

"I'm certainly not tiny now."

Mom holds the photo to her heart and sits on the futon. "You're not so big, Lola. Yeah, you're tall, but what's wrong with that? It's nice to be tall."

She's just being kind, just saying what a mother's supposed to say. I sit beside her and take another look at the photo in her hands. "I never felt like I fit in. It's like I don't belong in this family. You guys are so different from me. And you can't deny that I'm fat." I grab a handful of belly blubber and jiggle it.

Mom sighs and turns to face me. "You're a beautiful, smart, kind girl. Stop putting yourself down. Do you think Grandma Rose would like to hear you talk about yourself like that?"

Mom's never said anything like this to me before. Maybe it's because I've never told her how I feel. I can be withdrawn and usually keep my feelings to myself. Reluctantly, I admit that maybe it's me who doesn't try hard enough to be a part of this family.

"Be honest, Mom, she could stand to lose some weight." Eva smirks.

The truth of my sister's words instantly slams shut the tiny crack I'd allowed to open around my heart.

"Asshole," I mutter angrily as I get to my feet.

"What? It's true," she protests with a wicked smile.

I hip check her into the wall and stomp from the room. Behind me I hear Mom helping Eva to her feet and yelling at her at the same time.

Then again, maybe I don't want to be a part of this family.

Chapter Twenty-Three

By the time I climb into bed, I'm filled not only with grief over Grandma Rose, but hatred for my sister. Shutting off my brain is impossible and I toss and turn for hours. I imagine doing all kinds of mean things to Eva like flushing her cellphone, destroying her make-up suitcase, or stomping her head in. The only person who was ever able to free me from my rage is gone. Grandma Rose was the one I could talk to about anything and that included my evil sister. She could talk me down off the ledge every time and was always able to slip in something better for me to think about, before I even realized what happened.

The suffocating darkness of my room and the lonely quiet of the house drive me from my bed. My pain is monumental and my need to be near Gran is gargantuan.

After dressing, I grab my journal and stuff it into my satchel. I leave a note on the kitchen table, letting Mom and Dad know I've gone for a walk. The door squeaks, freezing me to the spot. I listen for a moment and, when I realize I haven't disturbed anyone, I sneak out into the early morning darkness.

The sun is not yet up and the cool air chills me to the bone. My loneliness is a solid, black thing, coiled around my throat like a boa constrictor. I tug at my collar to keep the panic from choking me. I run, trying to outpace my anxiety, but the banging of my heart feels too much like the panic I'm running from. I slow my pace, forcing long deep breaths and trudge on to fulfill a compulsion I cannot ignore.

Briefly, I think of Mom and hope when she gets my note she can understand and forgive me for once again not being there for her. My pain has driven me to such selfishness.

As I slip the key in the door to Gran's apartment, it's impossible to believe she won't be on the other side waiting for me with tea and burned cookies, and another crazy masterpiece on her easel. My heart shatters at the thought of never again hearing her voice, or her laughter or her words of wisdom. Of never looking into her eyes or feeling her touch, never ever again, as long as I live.

The apartment is black as pitch and eerily silent. I flick on the lights. Nothing has been touched. It feels as if she's on an errand and will soon burst through the door with her usual exuberance. I crumple to the floor at the entrance of the sunroom and cry. Soul shredding sobs make my shoulders heave. I cry and cry until I have no tears left. I am empty.

"Gran, I don't know if you can hear me, but I love you so much and I miss you. I want you to know you were the best grandmother *ever* and you've given me so many wonderful memories. I was blessed to have you in my life and I will keep you in my heart forever."

Does she hear me? I guess I'll never know. But I remember a story she'd told me not so long ago. It came out of the blue and now I wonder if Gran did have some kind of premonition of her impending death, or maybe it's just natural for eighty-year-olds to always be thinking of their mortality.

Gran explained that she and I are connected by an invisible cord. Though we can't see or feel it, it's there and can never be severed. It's the connection of love and she said that when she leaves the planet, the connection will still be there. We'll always be attached because of the strength of the love we have for each other. Although I never liked to hear her talk about death, I loved that story. It doesn't seem farfetched to me. I know for a fact that just because something can't be seen, it doesn't mean it's not there.

Finally, I pull myself to my feet and walk slowly around the tiny room. Canvases of all shapes and sizes are stacked one against the other, leaning on every wall. I flip through and find John Travolta and Katy Perry. I pull them free and select a couple others to take home with me.

Then I sit in my usual corner of the couch and pull the journal from my satchel.

"Gran, I hope you don't mind that I'm telling our secret," I say aloud. "It's a better story than the one I was writing and besides, no one but us and a couple of my friends will ever know it's true anyway."

I put pen to paper and write, ignoring the persistent ringing of my cellphone and the little beeps that tell me I've got a text message. The whole world can wait because nothing's more important than the story I'm telling. The words pour from me as if Gran is there beside me, whispering them in my ear.

Hours fly by like minutes and I continue until my fingers are cramped and my hand aches, and the rumble in my stomach cannot be ignored. I stop briefly to make a cup of tea and a peanut butter sandwich, and then I begin again.

By the time I close my journal, it's just past one in the afternoon. Unbelievably, I've written twenty-seven pages. I've never written so much in one day that I can actually be proud of. With a deep sense of contentment and accomplishment, I swing my feet onto the couch and snuggle against the soft cushions, letting my sleep-heavy lids fall. My breathing deepens and I drift into sleep.

A loud knock startles me and for a moment I'm frozen in place. It takes half a breath to remember where I am.

"Lola, you in there?" Dad calls.

I jump to my feet and run to let him in.

Strain and worry show on his face.

"Why the hell didn't you answer your phone?"

"I was writing," I say softly.

He sighs and rubs his jaw. "Your grandmother's wake is today. People will be arriving at the funeral home in less than an hour. Come on, let's get you home so you can change." He takes me by the arm.

"No, wait." I run back to the living room and gather up my belongings as well as the artwork and return with arms full.

Dad takes the pictures and helps me adjust my satchel across my shoulders. "Ready?"

"I'm ready to go, but I want to stay home."

He opens his mouth to protest, but I cut his words off. "I'll go to the funeral tomorrow, but please, Dad, I'm not ready to see Gran in a coffin yet. Not today, okay?"

"God damn it, Lola, your mom's not going to be happy about this."

"I know and I'm sorry to be such a disappointment. I'll be there tomorrow, okay?" There's a quiver in my voice and my eyes are wet with tears.

"Let's get you home." He takes my key and locks Gran's door.

* * * *

Once home, I check my phone. There are thirty-three texts from Charlie. I decide it would be easier to phone her rather than text back.

"Oh my God, are you okay? Why didn't you return any of my messages?" she asks in a flurry.

"I'm fine. I spent the day at Gran's."

"Oh." Her voice grows solemn. "My mom wants to know when visiting hours are for the wake."

"I'm not going to be there. The rest of my family is there now. I'm not sure when it's over tonight."

There's a long silence. Neither of us has been through anything like this before and it's awkward and uncomfortable.

"I'm going to the funeral tomorrow though, so I won't be at school until Thursday," I say finally. I think about asking if she's seen Jon but I can't go there yet, it's raw and embarrassing. No matter the circumstances, I still stood him up.

"I'll tell my mother we should go tomorrow then." There are tears in her voice.

"Thanks, Char, you're a great friend."

Charlie gives me a rundown of what I've missed in school and tells me she's collected my homework from all my teachers and that she'll bring it over later, after the funeral.

"Thanks again," I say.

"No problem, Lola." She pauses. "I love you."

Her words catch me off guard. "I... I love you too."

The connection goes dead.

It's time to type out my story and when I'm done, I print two copies; one for me and one for Gran. Then I fill out the online registration on my school's website, attach the electronic file and hit send.

Chapter Twenty-Four

I've never seen a dead body.

The casket is at the far end of the funeral parlor and I walk slowly, ominously, toward it. The overpowering scent of the flower-filled room makes me gag, yet I force air into my lungs to keep my heartbeat steady. I don't know what I'm more afraid of, seeing Gran in a coffin or disappearing.

Only close family are allowed in right now. Uncle Brian, his wife Maryanne and their boys Jimmy and Ryan are chatting with Mom and Dad. Gran's last surviving sister, my great aunt Mary and her family sit solemnly in a corner sniffling and sobbing. This is our last chance to see Gran and say good-bye before we head to the church for the funeral mass.

The gauze bandage is gone and my slightly scab-puckered tattoo is on display for the world to see. The scab will be gone in a day or two, but even in this state, I'm proud of it. It's my lasting connection to Gran, along with the invisible cord of love that runs from her heart to mine.

I'm holding a single red rose and a copy of my story that I've rolled up into a scroll and wrapped with a piece of purple satin, Gran's favorite color. When I get to the casket, the tears I'd bravely fought to control, stream down my cheeks.

Mom appears at my side and places a reassuring arm around my shoulders. "Let's kneel and say a prayer for her," she says.

We kneel together on a well-used green velour stand, but I can't pray, all I can do is stare. The woman in the coffin looks nothing like Gran. She looks like a wax figure. A small wave of relief floods me. It's better this way. It's better that it doesn't look like Grandma Rose in the coffin. Maybe I'll be able to fool myself into believing it's not really her.

The hair's wrong. It's too flat and old ladyish and they put blue eye shadow on her. She never wore blue eye shadow! I'm tempted to wipe it off. Gran would be so embarrassed. The outfit is fine, though. It reflects Gran's personality perfectly. She's wearing the navy blue dress she bought for her Cha Cha Cha on our last day together at the mall. It's not flashy. It looks like something she might have worn to a wedding or a special evening out.

I glance over to the foot of the coffin. I'd heard somewhere that's where the dead person's spirit stands during their funeral, so they can have a good look at who comes to pay their respects. I squint a little to try to catch a glimpse of Gran, but see nothing, not even a shimmering flicker of light. Then a thought strikes me... maybe she's just disappeared, like she used to; like I do. Maybe that's what dead really means – you're not really gone, just living in another realm where you're able to watch, but can't be heard or seen. This notion gives me comfort and I choose to believe it. I like thinking Gran's watching the entire goings on at her own funeral.

Mom whispers "Amen" and pulls me to my feet with her. "Lola, did you want to put the rose in with Gran?"

I pull my gaze from the foot of the casket to look at Mom. "Yes," I say and gently place the rose over Gran's folded hands, and then I tuck my rolled up story in beside her.

Mom throws me a look of surprise.

"It's just a story I wrote," I say quickly and turn away.

* * * *

After another fifteen minutes of hellish silent mourning, the funeral director finally opens the doors so the rest of the mourners can file in. Soon the room is full. There's talking, and crying and kissing of cheeks. I find the farthest corner to meld into and flirt with the idea of making myself disappear.

Then I see them, Charlie and Jon. I spot him first because he's so tall. My heart leaps and bangs against my ribs and a flush runs from my feet upwards until I feel my face redden.

Charlie scans the room and her eyes zone in on me like a laser beam. They both quickly head my way and stand in front of me like some sort of shield.

"Calm down, you're flickering," Charlie says, placing a hand on my shoulder.

I close my eyes and breathe deeply until my heartbeat slows. "Am I still here?" I whisper without opening my eyes.

"Yeah, you look solid now," Jon answers.

They each take a seat on either side of me and I open my eyes.

"I'm sorry about your Grandmother," Jon says. He's holding a small gift bag; light blue tissue paper blossoms from it.

"I'm sorry I stood you up," I reply.

He waves a hand in the air. "Please, you have nothing to be sorry about. Charlie explained it all."

"My mom wanted me to let you know she came to pay her respects last night," Charlie says, and then reaches in for a hug. "I'm so sorry about Grandma Rose."

"Thanks… for everything," I say and she squeezes me tighter.

"Let's have a look at the ink." She grabs my left hand, pushes up my sleeve and runs a finger gently across my still tender wrist. Jon leans in for a look too.

"It's a beautiful tribute," Charlie says.

"I think she'd be proud," adds Jon. "Oh, by the way…" He slips a hand into the pocket of his jeans. "Here."

He hands me a piece of paper.

"It's my number. We can keep in touch. Send me a text so I'll have yours too." Then he holds out the bag. "This is for you."

This brings a huge smile. I pull out the tissue and find a gorgeous dark brown leather-bound journal and a matching chocolate brown pen. The pen is heavy in my hand and it looks expensive.

"Wow, they're beautiful. I don't know what to say." I stare into his dark blue eyes until he looks away and gives an embarrassed smile. "It's absolutely perfect. How did you know?"

Jon eyes Charlie. "You've got a pretty good best friend there. She helped me pick them out. Besides, I see you writing all the time in English class."

"Thank you. I love them." I place my hand on his.

"I'm glad," he says, with a dimpled smile.

I just might be able to get through the rest of the day, after all.

Chapter Twenty-Five

After the funeral mass, Gran was cremated. Mom told me it was her wish and no matter how I feel about it, we all must respect Gran's last wishes. I can accept that, though I don't like to think about it. The idea of Gran being all burned up threatens to bring on another anxiety attack. It looms heavy on the horizon of my thoughts. Thankfully we didn't have to be there to witness it. The ashes will be presented to Mom and Uncle Brian in a few days. I'm not sure they know yet what to do with them.

I'm glad to be back at school so I can think of other things besides losing Gran. Once in homeroom, I slide into my usual spot and Jon sits beside me instead of in front of me.

"It's okay, I asked Patty if she'd trade," he explains.

Patricia Seaver has sat next to me since the first day of class. Don't know why, we're not exactly friends and we never talk. She's cheerleader material, skinny and flirty with a gleaming white-toothed smile and big blue eyes. I hate her because she makes me feel ugly. When Patty enters a moment later, she takes Jon's spot without so much as batting an eye.

Jon and I don't have much opportunity to talk during class, but it is nice having him near. I can hardly concentrate on what Mrs. Wright is saying because I'm so conscious of his presence. From the corner of my eye, I notice his gaze flicker in my direction, and a little half smile forming on his lips. A boy likes me! It feels so friggin' great.

After class, Jon walks me to my locker. "I've got something I want to ask you," he says, grinning.

Anything that makes Jon's dimples pop has to be good news. I smile back. "What is it?"

He clears his throat and his eyes flicker briefly from the floor, back to me. "Will you go to the graduation dance with me?"

It's all I can do to keep my feet planted on the floor. An urge threatens to overtake me, to jump up and down and squeal with joy, but I reign in my enthusiasm, choosing to keep it under wraps for later. "I'd love to." Suddenly, I love Mom for forcing me to get a dress.

Jon's still looking at me, his smile replaced by a more serious expression. He gently settles a hand on my cheek and kisses me; a sweet lingering kiss. His breath smells like peppermint and the familiar scent of his cologne engulfs me as I breathe him in. It's my favorite scent in the world.

Weak-kneed, I fall back against my locker.

He catches my elbow. "I didn't know my kisses had that much power," he says with a laugh.

I laugh too, to hide my embarrassment, but my cheeks burn, betraying me.

"See you at lunch?"

"By the oak tree," I answer.

He walks backwards down the hall, smiling and waving. I can't wait 'til he's out of sight so I can text Charlie. We're not allowed to use cellphones during school hours. Getting caught would mean a confiscated phone until the final bell rings, so I pivot toward my open locker and type quickly.

Jon asked me to the dance! ☺ ☺

No way! ☺ she replies almost instantly.

And something else happened…

Doooo tell.

He kissed me!!!!!!!!!!!!!'

OMG!!!! I'm really happy 4 u. ☺ ☺ ☺ ☺ The happy faces let me know she really means it.

All through my next class, I'm in dreamland. Not a single word the teacher says penetrates my brain. Jon's kiss has ignited something in me I didn't know existed. I'm going to start to eat healthier and maybe even work out. I want to be the best I can be. Not just for him, but for me.

* * * *

I'm the first to arrive at our lunch spot and Charlie comes running minutes later.

"Oh my god, I'm so happy for you!"

We do a little hop of joy and settle onto the ground looking around furtively to make sure there were no witnesses.

"And the dance. He asked you to the dance?" she asks excitedly.

I nod with furious abandon. Then realize Charlie will be dateless. "I'm sorry," I say.

She cocks her head and gives me a quizzical look. "What are you sorry for?"

Now it's awkward, but I say it nonetheless. "Because you don't have a date."

A sly smile forms on her lips. "Who said I didn't have a date?"

"You have a date?" I slap her knee. "Why didn't you tell me? Who is it?"

"Uh-ah. I'll never tell." She wags a finger.

"Really, you're not going to tell me?" I choose my next words carefully. "Do I know this person?" I don't say him or her because I'm still in the dark about Charlie's preferences.

"No, but you'll meet at the dance. And that's all I'm going to say about it, so don't bother trying to get any more out of me."

Charlie points behind me. "Here comes your *boyfriend*."

"Hey," says Jon, settling his lanky frame on the ground beside me.

With that one word I can tell instantly something's not right. Years of being hypersensitive have given me the same emotional barometer that Gran possessed.

"Something wrong?" I ask, doing my best to appear casual.

Jon heaves a sigh. "Just that asshole, Nino. It's nothing, don't worry about it."

"What did he do?" Charlie asks.

"You know how he is. He's just a dick." Jon undoes his shirt and gingerly pulls his left arm out of the sleeve to reveal a red mark that will no doubt soon morph into a purple bruise. "He punched me for no reason."

My stomach knots because I know there probably is a reason; that reason is me, and Jon just doesn't want to hurt my feelings.

"That shit-head," I say.

Charlie eyes me as Jon puts his shirt back on. "The plan," she mouths.

I shake my head and mouth back, "No."

"Guys, I'm right here. I can hear you. What's going on?" Jon says, fishing out his sandwich.

I narrow my eyes and shoot daggers at Charlie, but she ignores me. Her willingness to let Jon in on our plan surprises me. This is so not the Charlie I know. I suppose she trusts him now that they're all buddy-buddy since their bonding time while I was away.

"We've got a plan," says Charlie.

"A plan for what?" Jon asks.

"To get back at Nino."

Jon's brows lift with interest and he leans closer. "Spill. I want in."

Charlie explains while I eat. Jon's eyes widen with excitement and a huge smile fills his face. "It's perfect," he exclaims, thrusting a sandwich-filled hand in the air.

I'm a little nervous about Jon knowing; especially since I've never really agreed to do it. Frankly, I don't think I've got the guts, or the will to go through with it.

"There are only a couple more weeks left of school, and then we'll all be going our separate ways. Why not just forget about him. He's not worth the effort," I say. But they're now talking to each other and ignoring me, while they put the final polish on "the plan."

"Ah, come on, Lola, he deserves what he's got coming to him," Charlie says. "We need you or it just won't happen." She looks at me with pleading eyes. Jon adds pouty lips and hands held up in prayer.

"He needs to be knocked back down to earth and we can do that," Jon says. "He thinks his shit don't stink just because he's the top senior athlete."

"Yeah, really," says Charlie. "Big deal, so he's the captain of the lacrosse team. Big shit."

"And the football and basketball teams," Jon adds in a reluctant tone.

"All he really is," Charlie says, "is a bully and nothing more."

"And I bet he wins the athletic scholarship award." Jon punches his own knee, and then grimaces. "Life's not fair. Only the assholes of the world seem to get ahead. Come on, Lola, this is our last chance to punish him for everything he's done over the years."

I sit in contemplation for a moment, and then heave a sigh. They're right, and despite losing Gran, I'm feeling something I haven't felt in probably forever – hope. I'm actually hopeful about my future. No doubt Jon has a little something to do with that. But my recent sense of contentment worries me. In order to pull off the plan, it might be hard to bring to the surface those feelings necessary to make myself invisible. I could always try to use the good feelings. Gran said either/or would work, yet the horrible, despicable ones; the ones that bring tears to my eyes and churning knots to my stomach seem to work best.

"I have to think about it, guys. I mean, what would happen if I couldn't make myself disappear? Or, God forbid, I reappear in the middle of it." I flush, thinking about the coffee shop episode with Jon.

"All right," Jon says. "Think about it."

"But we're not done talking about this just yet," Charlie adds.

Chapter Twenty-Six

For the last three days I've jogged around the block. Well, maybe jogging's not exactly the right word. I've walked fast around the block, several times. It made me feel like I was going to puke up a lung, but I did it and I'm proud. I've also by-passed the fries in the school cafeteria and I only eat half my regular helping of dinner, which frankly isn't all that hard since I'm pretty damn sick of stir-fry. I don't know what I weigh and I don't want to find out, so I've avoided the scale, but I'm delighted that my jeans feel a teensy bit baggy. It's not a lot but it's a start.

Today's Sunday and what used to be my favorite day of the week is now a dark empty space of a day. A day with a hole in it, much like my heart. But I feel strong enough to handle putting up Gran's paintings in my room and think it only fitting that I do it on a Sunday. Dad's not much of a handyman and I had to scrounge around the garage to find a few nails. I hammer them into the drywall with one of Mom's shoes that has a good, solid wedge heel.

Katy Perry is going over my bed and John Travolta on the opposite wall. Gran's all around me now. I sit cross-legged in the middle of my bed and smile, drinking in her creative spirit. The hole is still there, but it's a tiny bit smaller now that it's got a little bit of Gran in it.

Mom's at the hairdresser. She asked if I wanted to join her and for the first time ever, I actually thought about saying yes, but common sense prevailed. The risk of coming out of that funky salon she goes to looking like a fat Amy Winehouse was too great.

After putting up the paintings, I spend the rest of the day doing homework and texting Jon while he's at work. Charlie's working too, but she's not allowed to text at her job. They make all the teenagers leave their cellphones at home. I think that's unfair. It sounds like discrimination to me, but Charlie needs the job to help out at home and even if she snuck it in, I wouldn't dare text her in case I get her into trouble.

Later today, Mom, Dad and Uncle Brian are going to collect Gran's ashes. Mom says they've decided to bury her urn in Grandpa Ken's plot at Holy Family Cemetery. Mom asked if I wanted to be there for the burial, but I decided to stay home. It was bad enough seeing Gran in a coffin, I can't bear to see her put into the ground, even though I know that's not really Gran any more, and that she's in a better place.

Unfortunately, Eva will be home too. She broke up with her boyfriend a couple of days ago and all she does is mope around the house. I wish I could tell her about Jon and rub in the fact that I have an *almost* boyfriend and she has no one. But I don't want to remind her about him just yet. She hasn't bothered to ask about Jon since our date was cancelled the night of Gran's heart attack. I'm sure, as self-absorbed as Eva is, she's all but forgotten him.

I'm surprised at how well I've been holding up. Without Jon and Charlie in my life, I'm sure I'd be a mess. It's true what they say, "God never closes a door without opening a window." Gran used to say that all the time. Jon is my window.

When evening rolls around, it's just me and my evil sister. Mom and Dad left us money for a pizza. Of course, Eva called in the order and asked for all her favorite toppings, leaving me to pick off the mushrooms and disgusting green olives from my slice.

We get comfortable on the couch with our dishes and Eva grabs the remote before I have a chance. I heave a sigh and settle in to watch *A Baby's Story* and then *Say Yes to the Dress*. Gawd, could two sisters be any more different?

After just one slice of pizza instead of my usual four, I down two large glasses of water instead of Pepsi.

"You on a diet or something?" Eva asks without turning from the TV.

"No," I say quickly.

"Yes, you are."

"I'm just not hungry."

Eva swivels around and gives me the once over. "It's that boy you were supposed to go out with. I can tell. You're in love with this loser and you think if you can drop a few hundred pounds, he might ask you out again."

Eva's got more brains than I gave her credit for. Looks like I've sold her short. "You're just jealous 'cause Kevin dumped your ass." I raise a brow and smile with satisfaction. That one had to have cut to the bone.

"You're still fat, and you'll always be fat." Her lips curve into a hateful sneer, dowsing my smile. I want more than anything to punch her teeth down her throat.

"Your hair looks like a couple of rats have made a home in it and you wear too much make-up," I retort. "You look like a friggin' hooker, that's why Kevin dumped you. And you're stupid. You're just a stupid girl who only knows about shallow things that don't matter, like what shade of bronzer goes with which type of complexion."

Tears spring to her eyes and I'm glad for it.

"What about you? You don't belong in this family. No one loves you. Mom and Dad pretend to because you're their misfit daughter, but the only person who loved you is d-e-a-d, dead. Gran ain't ever coming back and now there's no one in the whole world who loves you."

Her words slice like shards of freshly shattered glass and I double over feeling as if I've been punched in the gut. My heart flutters hard, stealing my breath.

"Ahhh!" Eva cries and scrambles crab-like to the farthest end of the couch. "Oh, my God!"

My heart settles to a slow rhythmic beat – that and Eva's reaction tells me I've vanished.

Rage still rushes through me and my fingers curl into fists. I decide to use my invisible time to my advantage.

Eva's still staring at the spot where I was when I disappeared, but now I'm standing in front of her. I grab a handful of her hair and yank so hard she slips from the couch, landing on the floor with an inelegant *clunk*. Then I kick her hard, in the ribs and finish with a good twisting pinch to the fleshy part of her right arm.

Eva's eyes are wide with horror. "Stop, stop!" she screams, swiping wildly at the air.

I peer down at her. She's pitiful with her black-ringed eyes wet with tear-smudged mascara. I'm ashamed. Although she deserves it, we'll never be friends, so what's the point of perpetuating this. It's better to just keep away. We're too different to ever get along.

I turn to walk away, leaving her crying on the floor.

"W...w...where did you go just now?" Eva asks in a frightened whisper.

"I'm back?" I ask, not quite sure.

She nods and wraps her arms around her drawn up knees. Her mascara now runs in black streaks down her cheeks and her hair is a lopsided mess.

I walk over to her and hold out a hand.

She flinches and looks truly petrified, making me feel worse than ever.

"I'm sorry," I say, but she still doesn't take my hand.

"What *are* you?"

With undignified grace, I sit beside her. "I don't know. Guess I'm just some kind of freak."

"It's happened before?"

"A few times, but I'm getting better at controlling it."

"Do Mom and Dad know?"

I shake my head slowly, suddenly fearful she'll tell. "Don't tell," I say sternly.

"But they should know…"

"If you tell on me, to anyone, anyone at all, I'll come into your room and take a video of you when you're dancing around singing, like I *know* you do, and I'll put it on YouTube. *And* since I'll be invisible, you'll never know when I show up to do it. Plus, I can still beat the shit out of you anytime I want, since you won't see me coming."

Eva hugs her knees tighter and wipes tears and snot from her face with a sleeve. "I won't tell."

Chapter Twenty-Seven

Two weeks until graduation and the dance. Butterflies dance in my belly and thoughts of Jon make my heart sing. My only wish is that Gran could be here to share in my joy. I'm happier than I've been since I was a kid; before I knew how hard life really is.

Not much real work's getting done during these last few days of school and I'm surprised when Mrs. Wright asks me to stay behind after homeroom English. I've handed in all my major assignments and next week is exams, so I can't imagine what she has to say.

Jon waves bye from the doorway and calls, "See you at lunch."

I smile and wave back while Mrs. Wright waits patiently. How many young loves must she have witnessed over her career? She's old. I'd guess close to retirement, with steel gray hair, cut short, but not boyish. There's enough length to give her a slightly feminine look. Although she wears no make-up and always dresses in a burgundy blazer and black pleated dress pants. Man, she must have a closet filled with burgundy blazers and black pleated pants. At least I hope so. I'd hate to think she's wearing the same outfit every day. She's tiny and makes me feel like Godzilla. I always slouch horribly when I'm near her.

"Sit down, Lola; we have a few minutes 'til the next class starts. I'll give you a note so you won't be marked late." She gives me a gap-toothed smile.

"Thanks," I sit, relieved I'm no longer staring down at the top of her head.

She picks up a folder and perches on the edge of her desk. "I've got your submission for the creative writing scholarship award and I have to say, Miss Savullo, you're a wonderful writer. The imagination, the descriptive narrative, the *emotional impact*." She sighs and looks skyward crushing my story to her chest. "It's truly incredible." Her eyes find mine. "Do you want to be a writer? Or an English teacher?" She says the latter with an enthusiastic tone.

A smile unfurls across my face and suddenly I'm drifting on cloud nine. "I want to be a writer," I say excitedly.

"Then you *must* follow your dream." She drives home her point by leaning forward and wagging a dainty finger. "There are quite a few contenders for the scholarship. I'm really quite impressed with the talent this year. I'm having one-on-one sit downs with everyone who has a story entered, to let you each know what marvellous jobs you've done, and to wish... you... luck." The final three words emerge in a staccato of pointed emphasis.

My lips thin to a line in disappointment and I let out a huff of air through my nose. There are others? Others who are just as good? Others who are just as talented? My shoulders deflate. If I were a turtle, I'd be tucked into the safety of my shell right now.

"Thanks, Mrs. Wright, I'd better get going."

She doesn't seem to notice my waning enthusiasm, and continues to beam at the enormity of the writing talent among her students, as if she's the sole reason for it. She writes my note in an unbelievably neat script; no doubt, the result of the perfect combination of old lady and English teacher; that is Mrs. Wright. "Here you are Miss Savullo. Good luck with the scholarship."

I take the note, plaster on a smile and leave.

* * * *

Lunch rolls around and I find Charlie under the oak waiting for me. Before sitting, I scan for Jon.

"I don't think he's coming," Charlie says.

"How do you know?"

She sets her half-eaten bologna sandwich down on the brown paper lunch bag on her knee. "I saw him with Nino and Tyler."

"*What?* When?"

"Just now. At Nino's locker. I didn't want to have to tell you this, but I heard Jon ask to eat lunch with them."

"He wouldn't go with them, at least not willingly. Did it look like he was scared? Did Nino push him around or yell at him?" None of this makes any sense. I try to quell my sudden panic. There has to be a reason.

"No. He looked happy to go with them. I'm sorry." Charlie takes another bite of her sandwich and a swig of Pepsi.

"I don't believe it. You saw how Nino treats Jon. He punches him and puts him in head locks and..."

"But that's how guys are. They horse around like that all the time. I wouldn't worry about it, it doesn't mean he doesn't like *you* any more," she says around the edges of a belch.

I'm not buying what she's selling. From the look in Charlie's eyes, I can tell she's worried too. "That's how it feels." I walk to a garbage can and throw my lunch away. "I'm going to the cafeteria to see for myself."

"Wait, I'll come too." Charlie jumps to her feet and links her arm through mine. Together we march into the noisy, chaos-filled cafeteria of Maple Ridge Secondary School.

"Look who it is," Nino hollers from across the room.

I will my feet to move until Charlie and I are standing directly in front of Nino, Tyler, Julia and Jon.

"Jonny-boy," Nino snarls, "looks like your girlfriend's here to see you."

"You a chubby chaser, Jon?" Tyler asks, nudging Jon with a shoulder.

Jon doesn't look at me. He focuses on his hands that are resting on his bobbing knees; it's his nervous habit. His cheeks burn in red splotches and sweat beads on his brow.

"Why don't you sit down and join us, ladies, or is it offensive to call a dyke a lady?" Nino says, eyeing Charlie.

"Let's go." Charlie pulls me away.

"Hey, why don't you show us your disappearing act?" Nino calls as we walk away.

I stop dead, blood draining to my feet.

Charlie takes hold and with a determined yank, drags me out of the cafeteria and into the bathroom.

I just make it into a stall before the fluttering in my chest tells me I've disappeared.

"Lola? You okay?"

"No," I answer but I know full well she can't hear me.

"Lola?"

I concentrate on the stall door, give it a good kick, and see Charlie's red sneakers leap back in surprise. She inches forward. "You gone?"

Again I bang the door. "Okay. Good job with the kicking by the way." There's a tinge of excitement in her voice. "I'll just wait then. Let me know when you think you're back."

I perch on the edge of the chipped black plastic toilet seat and try to calm myself with deep breathing, but it's useless, I'm too upset.

Charlie peeks under the door. "Not back yet," she mutters more to herself than me.

The bathroom door creaks open and the room is suddenly flooded with the sounds of the hallway as someone walks in.

"Get out," Charlie commands.

An indignant huff echoes through the room and the girl, whoever she was, leaves.

"Take deep breaths, Lola. Forget about them. Guys are assholes. They all end up hurting you, eventually."

How could Jon do this to me? I'd confided in him my deepest secret and he told my enemies. Why does everybody hate me? And why do I have to keep disappearing. God, it's really starting to get on my nerves.

I squeeze my eyes shut and imagine my feet planted firmly on the floor, holding me in place like the roots of a tree. Then I visualize a stream of white light funnelling through me, from the crown of my head, down my spine and into my feet. I'm not sure where all this is coming from; perhaps from one of those new age meditation videos I used to watch years ago.

Something's happening.

It's subtle, as if a weight has been lifted.

My breath escapes me in one big relieved *whoosh*.

I'm back and I know it.

With a palm I bang on the stall door and Charlie's upside down smiling face appears. "Welcome back."

I click open the door. "I think I've discovered a way to bring myself back faster."

"That's great. What did you do?"

"Just planted my feet, really felt them solid on the ground and imagined a flow of energy running through me and into the floor."

"Good, the more control over your ability, the better you'll feel about it."

Despite my new discovery, I can't manage to work up any excitement over it. "I can't stay at school a minute longer, Char. I've got to get out of here."

She slaps my back and leads me out the door. "I'm with ya. How 'bout we go to the mall?"

"Sounds good to me."

We make a brief stop at our lockers to grab our knapsacks, wallets and cellphones and ten minutes later we're sitting on the 64B.

The whole way there my phone buzzes incessantly. "Jon's texting me." I hold the phone up to show Charlie.

"What's he saying?"

"He's sorry and he wants to explain."

"What are you going to do?"

I power off the phone. "That's what I'm going to do. Nothing he can say will ever make up for what he just did to me."

Despite the heaviness in my heart, Charlie and me manage a little fun. We try on clothes and have a bite in the food court. Then we stop in at U-Nique Tattoos and Piercings to say hi to Ben, but he's not in and Billy's too scary to talk to, even for Charlie, so we hurry out.

It's a relief to spend the afternoon away from school and with my best friend.

"Thanks for this," I say as we walk through the mall, enjoying a frozen yogurt – an extra-large chocolate with two spoons. "I guess you're right about guys. They do end up hurting you."

"Yeah, I see it every day in my mother's face and in how hard she has to work to make ends meet. My dad's an asshole, and not only does she have to pay for it, I do too. There's no future for me. I have to get a full-time job right after graduation to help out."

Charlie's words make me wonder if that's why she is the way she is. I want so much to ask if she prefers girls to boys, but I don't have the courage. I guess I'll just have to wait 'til the grad dance. That notion brings an unpleasant thought. I guess I don't have a date any more.

"What are you going to do tomorrow when you see Jon?" Charlie asks.

I lift one shoulder in a shrug. "Ignore him. It shouldn't be too hard, school's almost over and then I'll never have to see him again. At least we weren't boyfriend and girlfriend yet," I say knowing that's no consolation. He still managed to break my heart.

"Guess that's the right thing to do. The days will pass and soon we'll be out of school. Well, at least I'll be. You're still going to university."

I sigh. "Yeah, I sure hope it's different there."

"I think it will be. You'll have a fresh start. You can reinvent yourself."

"I don't think there's any use in that. I am what I am, and *who* I am." I think about what Grandma Rose told me in the hospital – I've got to find a way to love myself. That seems like the answer to all my problems.

The question is how?

Chapter Twenty-Eight

I make it home just in time to intercept the pre-recorded message from my school. The voice on the other end lets me know which periods were missed by Lola Savullo. Which is pretty stupid really, since every kid at Maple Ridge High knows to expect the call and grab the phone before the unsuspecting parent catches a whiff of guilt from their school-skipping teenager. I erase the call history when I hang up. I'll write myself a note, sign Mom's name and take it to the attendance office tomorrow.

Dinner's uneventful and quiet. Eva steals furtive glances and I meet her gaze with a stern glare and a slow shake of my head. She looks away. Size has always been my one advantage over Eva. She knows I can pummel her into the ground as easily as swatting a mosquito, but now I have more ammo. Now, there's not just fear reflected in her eyes, but terror. I grin inwardly and secretly wish I could gloat.

I've played around with the thought of letting my secret out. The power I'd have over my family would be satisfying, but it wouldn't feel right. I know the kind of girl I am, and it's not the power hungry, "I'm going to crush you unless I get my way" kind. I'm the "don't look at me… I wish I were invisible" sort of girl. After all, isn't this how it all started in the first place? Pretty ironic, actually.

After dinner I go to my room and toss my still silent cellphone onto my desk. It's a relief to be incommunicado. I'm in my own little world for a while with no distractions.

After plucking a novel from my shelf, *Club Dead*, book three of the Sookie Stackhouse series, I make myself comfortable on my bed to read for a while.

A moment later, Eva trounces up the stairs, her door clicks shut; probably on her laptop, instant messaging her loser friends. I'm just glad she's staying out of my way.

The sounds of Mom cleaning up after dinner and Dad watching television filter up to my room and I marvel at how life goes on, despite loss, hurt and the injustices of the world.

A moment later, the doorbell breaks my concentration. Dad's heavy footfalls echo through the hallway as he makes his way to the door.

I elbow myself up, cock an ear and listen.

Dad's deep voice carries well, and along with it, another voice filters through my bedroom door. It's Jon!

"Lola!" Dad calls.

Unsure what to do, I jump to my feet. I have no choice but to face him.

"Lola, someone's here to see you!" he calls again, his voice a little sing-songy.

I creak open my door. "Okay, be right there."

Eva's door inches open and our eyes meet from across the hall. I throw her a nasty look. *Nosy bitch.* She turns her nose up in seeming disgust and clicks the door shut again.

I head downstairs, sucking in deep breaths all the way.

Jon's standing in the front entrance, tall and handsome in a dark gray sweatshirt and baggy jeans, a single red rose in his hand.

He holds out the flower. "This is for you."

With arms folded tightly across my chest, I narrow my eyes. "I don't want it," I say through gritted teeth.

Dad's smile fades and Mom, who had taken a few steps toward us, quickly returns to the kitchen, now with Dad right behind her.

"Will you come for a walk with me?"

"Why would I go anywhere with you?"

The hand holding the rose falls. "I know I don't deserve for you to even talk to me, but if you'd let me explain…"

I hold up a hand to still him. "I don't want to hear your excuses. Nothing you can say will justify what you did to me today."

"What if I told you I did it to save you and Charlie?"

That catches my attention and the next round of cruel words die in my throat. "Okay, let's walk."

The late afternoon is warm and the signs of summer bloom everywhere. Trees are filling in with dense foliage and flowers brighten the front yards of each house we pass.

"Don't you want this?" he asks, holding the rose out to me again.

I shake my head. "Where do you want to go?"

He lets the flower drop to the sidewalk. "I don't care where we go, just as long as you listen to me."

"Start talking." I walk at a good clip.

"Julia told me that Nino was going to beat you up after graduation and that he was going to do something... *worse* to Charlie."

My heart launches into my throat and I stop dead. "What?"

"It's true. She told me right before lunch. I didn't believe it at first, but you shoulda seen the look on her face. She cried when she told me. Julia's not all bad. I used to think Nino was an okay guy, that he was just a bit of a jerk, but I know better now. He's dangerous, Lola. It's up to me to protect you and Charlie and I'll do whatever it takes." Tears stand in his eyes.

"What was he going to do to Charlie?" I ask slowly, not sure I really want to know.

Jon brings a hand to his forehead and rubs his temples. "You know," he says in a hesitant whisper.

"No, I don't know. Tell me."

He begins to walk away and I have to jog to catch up with him. "Please, tell me."

A frown creases his forehead. "Something bad… because she's a lesbian."

A sick feeling ferments in the pit of my stomach. I clutch at his arm. "Are you sure? Are you 100% certain?"

"Pretty certain."

"Then we've got to go to the police."

"What can they do? Nothing's happened yet. I think our best bet is to make sure nothing does. That's why I want to get close enough to watch his every move."

"And then what? What can you do by yourself if he does try something? And what about Tyler? Is he in on this?"

"No. He's too chicken shit. This is all Nino. If he did go through with it, that's the only time we could call the police."

I spot the park up ahead, the same one where Nino, Tyler and Julia called me names and I disappeared.

Grabbing a fistful of Jon's sweatshirt, I pull him along with me. "Let's sit and talk."

We find a bench far from the playing, screaming children.

My mind reels. Is Nino really that cruel? He's certainly capable of beating me up, but what evil did he have planned for Charlie? I picture my friend, slim and fine boned. Sure, she looks tough, but I know better. Beneath the rough exterior is a warm, loving and kind girl. What would it do to her if she were violated? Her life would be shattered. I can't bear to think of it.

My thoughts return to Jon, my anger at him still boiling. "But why did you have to tell him my secret?"

"Because I needed Nino to trust me. It was the only thing I could think of. I have to know what he's planning in order to protect you and Charlie."

"That was *my* secret." I bite my quivering lip.

"I know and I'm so sorry, Lola. Please forgive me." His eyes are big and pleading and despite my resolve, my anger falls away. There is truth and kindness reflected there.

"Is he really going to *hurt* Charlie?" I can't make myself say the word Jon and I are both trying to avoid.

"I really think so but don't worry, I won't let that happen." He slides an arm around me and pulls me close. I let him, and rest my head on his shoulder. "And I'd never let him lay a finger on you," he says, caressing my cheek.

My fear is stronger for Charlie than for myself. If necessary, I can vanish and get away, but not poor Charlie. She'd have no choice but to endure whatever vile act Nino is contemplating.

Curiosity nudges me. "What did Nino say when you told him I could disappear?"

"He laughed. He didn't believe it and just thought you were nuts."

"Do Tyler and Julia know too?"

"Yeah, but they don't believe it either."

I pull away to face Jon. "Then we're going to have to prove it to Nino. The others don't matter, but Nino needs to be convinced."

Jon's eyebrows shoot up. "Why?"

"We have to, if our plan's going to work."

A slow smile forms on his lips. "You're on board with the plan?"

"I am now."

Chapter Twenty-Nine

It's Monday and the final bell has rung.

"Can we talk?" I ask Charlie.

"What about?"

It was tough going, but I'd managed to keep to myself all day what Jon told me yesterday. There were so many times I wanted to tell her about Nino's plans. But why spoil her school day? The rest of the day will be ruined soon enough.

"There's something important I need to tell you," I reply.

"We can talk on the bus," she says, walking away to stand in the bus line.

I grab her shoulder and spin her toward me. "We can take the late bus. Or walk home. What I have to say is private and I don't want anyone to hear."

She studies my eyes, as if searching for a clue, then shrugs. "Okay."

Charlie follows me to the courtyard behind the school, and my stomach twists because of the words I must say.

We settle at one of the many picnic tables strewn throughout the courtyard. We're alone and I haven't told Charlie that Jon will be meeting up with us shortly. She doesn't know we're friends again.

"So, what's so important?" There's a hint of worry in her voice, and she's clutching herself, as if bracing for bad news. It kills me to know soon she'll have a worry; a burden to carry. Soon she'll be scared, and then she'll be furious.

"I found out why Jon was with Nino at lunch."

Her eyes flash with interest and she leans closer. "Why?"

Panic swells in my throat and for a moment I'm not sure I can spit out the words.

"What? Tell me." An unsure smile flickers.

Unable to meet her gaze, I sigh and look away. "Nino has plans to hurt us the night of the grad dance." Without waiting for her questions, I continue, "He was going to beat me up and… *assault* you."

She utters a humorless bark of laughter. "What? Whadda ya mean?"

"I mean," I whisper even though we're alone, "word is Nino has plans to… to do something unspeakable to you."

"Who said?" Her face flushes and there's a tremble in her bottom lip.

"Julia told Jon. Tyler told her and I guess she's got a bit of a conscience."

"Really? This is *really* true?" Now her face shrivels in a look of pain.

I rest a soothing hand on her arm. "Jon won't let it happen though, so we don't have to worry."

She gets to her feet and sways unsteadily for a moment, then crumples to the pavement.

"Charlie!" I squat beside her and rub comforting circles on her back while she cries. "Are you okay?"

When she finally looks at me, she's pale-faced and trembling. "That's the worst thing he could ever do to me."

"It's not going to happen." I move over and pull her into my arms.

She clings to me and hot tears fall onto my shoulder. "What did I ever do to him?"

"Don't worry, we'll make him pay." I lift her chin with a finger and find her gaze. "I want to go ahead with the plan. That's why I wanted to meet here with you. Jon's coming too."

"Okay," she whispers, sounding like a frightened child. "But are you sure about Jon?"

"Yes, he's only hanging out with Nino and Tyler to see what he can find out, so he can protect us."

She nods, seemingly satisfied with my answer. We sit in silence, each thinking our own thoughts until Jon jogs up.

"I guess you told her," he says, eyeing Charlie, who's now sitting cross-legged on the pavement, fingers laced through fistfuls of hair.

"Charlie, you've got nothing to worry about," he says. "I won't let anything happen to you, or to Lola." He offers a hand and she takes it. He pulls her to her feet and she falls into him for a hug.

Surprise lights his face and he pats her back, throwing me a look of astonishment.

"Thank you," she says and pulls away.

Jon nods and gives an awkward smile. "No prob. Umm, we have to make sure no one sees us together for the next little while. It has to look like I'm their friend." Jon turns to me. "I figure the middle of next week will be the best time to prove to Nino that you really can disappear."

"Wait, whaddaya mean?" Charlie asks. "Why does Lola have to prove it?"

"If the plan's going to work, we have to show Nino that Lola really can disappear, or he won't take our threats seriously," Jon explains. "We have to scare the shit out of him to get him to do what we want."

"But I thought you already told him she could vanish."

"Yeah, I did, but he didn't believe it. Really, think about it, who would? So we've got to show him."

"How are we gonna do it?" I ask.

"I've been thinking, and maybe I can ask him to meet me right here in the courtyard after school, and you can be waiting for us," he suggests. "I won't let him go until you show him what you can do."

"I've got a better idea," I say, shaking my head. "Let *me* ask him to meet me here, alone. If I feel the fear

139

and anxiety for real, I'll wink out right away and I won't have to focus and concentrate, which takes time."

Charlie reaches out a hand. "Too dangerous."

"Yeah," Jon adds, "I think so too."

"Okay then, what if you guys wait there." I point to our oak tree. It's huge and ancient and two people can easily hide behind its massive trunk. "Besides, what can he do to me if he can't see me?"

They exchange a look, then Jon shrugs and Charlie nods.

"Okay," Jon says finally. "We'll be right there watching the whole time."

"What if Tyler and Julia show up too?" Charlie asks.

"I'll tell Julia to make sure Tyler doesn't go with Nino," Jon answers.

"And you're sure we can trust her?"

"Yeah, I don't know if Lola told you, but she's the one who told me about Nino's plan in the first place."

Charlie sneers. "What if Tyler's thinking of getting in on the action?"

"Judging from everything I've heard, this is all Nino. Don't get me wrong, Tyler's an asshole, he knows what Nino wants to do and he's doing nothing to talk him out of it, but I think he's too scared to join in."

"How do you know you're not being taken for a ride here? I mean they know you're close to me and Lola, why would they suddenly trust you?"

Jon heaves a sigh. "They don't know Julia told me about the plan, so as far as they're concerned I have no idea what they've got planned. Plus I made it look like I was on the outs with Lola. Trust me, it hasn't been easy. I want to fuckin' punch their faces in, but I've got to be convincing so they let me hang out with them." He pauses, tapping pursed lips. "Actually, why don't we stage something? I can act like an asshole and call you guys some names to really make them believe I'm on their side."

"Good idea," I hear myself say, but my gut clenches at the thought of it.

"And how do you know Julia's not going to ruin everything by telling her boyfriend what's really going on?" Charlie asks.

"I haven't told Julia about *our* plan, and as much of a bitch as she is, she doesn't want you to get… hurt."

"So she's fine with me getting beaten up?" I huff.

Jon shrugs. "God, I hate to say it, but I guess so."

* * * *

For the rest of the week I avoid Jon like the plague. I even sit on the other side of the class in homeroom. I throw him dirty looks at every opportunity, even if no one's looking. He does the same. We're playing our parts like pros.

Jon eats lunch with Nino, Tyler and Julia, and Charlie and I eat outside under the oak tree, even in the rain. We're determined to do this thing right. Hatred, anger and a need for justice drive us.

The day of our staged fight comes quickly and I'm scared. Charlie's eager and excited, and for the life of me, I can't figure out why.

The final bell rings and we head outside to wait for our bus. I see Jon and the others from the corner of my eye and suck in deep soothing breaths. "You ready?" I whisper to Charlie. "They're coming."

A wicked smile forms on her lips. "Bring it."

I pretend not to see them.

"Since when are cows allowed on the bus?" says Jon and though I know he doesn't mean what he says, his words still sting.

Nino laughs. "Good one, man."

I turn to see him slap Jon on the back. There's a scowl on Jon's face and he really looks like he hates my guts. Tyler stands with an arm draped over Julia's shoulder. She may have done us a favor, but the glare on her face looks pretty friggin' real too.

"Leave me alone, asshole," I say in a venom-infused voice. Jon moves closer and stops to throw a look at his fake friends. "You know why I don't hang out with her any more?"

"Why, man?" Tyler asks.

"Because they want to be alone. Two fuckin' man-hating lesbos."

Charlie wheels around, and spits in Jon's face.

"Bitch!" he snarls, and shoves her backwards.

She almost falls, but regains her feet at the last moment.

The whole scene is so real, it steals my breath. My heart beats hard against my ribs and I turn and run.

Charlie follows, jogging beside me. "Take it easy," she soothes. "Our bus will be here soon. Please, Lola, don't wink out. It wasn't real."

"I know," I say between lungfuls of air. "It's not real. It's not real." My words are my mantra.

Before the late bus arrives, I've managed to get myself under control. There will be no disappearing.

"Did you have to spit on him?" I say as Charlie and I take a seat.

"It had to look real."

"It did."

"So you think they bought it?" Charlie says, gathering her expression into a smile.

"It scared the shit out of me and I *knew* it was fake, so yeah, I think they bought it."

Charlie leans back satisfied. "Step one done, now onto the next. It's all you now, missy. Put on that author hat and write up a good speech. Do you need my help, or do you remember everything we talked about?"

"I think I'll be okay. I've been making notes."

"Hurry up and write it. We're running out of time. Next week is exams and then graduation the following Friday."

I know only too well what the next few days hold.

* * * *

When I walk through my front door, my cell's buzzing. It's Jon. He wants to make sure I'm all right and that he didn't hurt Charlie. Even though it was just an act, his words bring me relief.

U gonna write tonight? he texts.

Yup, I reply.

Good – text u later.

After dinner, I jog around the block, twice. It's back to my routine. I grab a shower and then settle in to write Nino's new speech, the one we have to convince him to read during the presentation of his athletic scholarship award on graduation day.

Chapter Thirty

Class started a few minutes ago and Nino and I are alone in the corridor. All the girls think Nino's a god: broad-shouldered, muscular and tall. But I hate him more than I've ever hated anyone. So, to me, he's not just ugly, he's hideous. He's at the end of the hallway and as I walk toward him, I take long deep breaths, in through my nose and out through my mouth. It's become my routine, my habit. The steady rhythm of my heart comforts me, letting me know I'm in control – no winking out until I decide to. Getting Nino to do what I want will be easy. I've been practising; running the words over and over in my mind, until they're all I can think about.

He's tugging on something; his knapsack, I think, trying to free it from his locker. I reach out and give his shoulder a quick tap. He turns, a smile flashes, but is quickly replaced with disappointment and a look of disgust. "What do you want, pig?" He spits the last word at me like a dagger.

Drawing my shoulders back, I straighten to my full height. "You're a bastard. A good-for-nothing piece of shit and a waste of flesh." I inject as much venom as I can muster.

His chocolate eyes flash in anger and he lunges at me, making me stumble backwards, almost losing my balance. He barks a wicked laugh. "Get the fuck out of my face you fat, ugly bitch." He turns back to his locker and his wedged knapsack.

"No, not this time." I stab him hard in the ribs with a finger. "Meet me after school in the courtyard," I say through gritted teeth.

His eyes widen and his mouth hangs open.

"If you're man enough, that is." A slow smile of satisfaction blossoms on my lips, as I turn on my heel and saunter off.

"Well?" Charlie asks when I round the corner.

I grab her arm and pull her with me. "Let's go."

When we're far enough away, I let out my breath and a nervous laugh. "You should've seen the look on his face. I shocked the hell out of him."

"But do you think he'll show?"

"Yeah, I think so, but I'm more worried about Jon holding up his end of the bargain and getting Julia to keep Tyler away."

"Hope you didn't come across as a psycho. Maybe he'll be too scared to show. He might think you're gonna shoot him or stab him or somethin'."

"Ha!" I laugh, but realize she may be right. "Hope I didn't overdo it. I guess we'll just have to wait and see." I check the time on my cellphone. "We'll know in two hours."

We skip class and go across the street to the strip mall to grab a tea at the donut shop. The place is crowded with students. Keeping butts in seats in the classroom is a losing battle this time of year. We sip tea, snack on chocolate croissants and talk about anything but Nino and what's to come. The hours pass like days, until finally it's time to head back to school and to the courtyard.

I text Jon on the way. *Where R U?*

At our spot.

On the way.

Charlie and I pick up our pace and separate when we hit school property. I scan the crowd of students waiting for buses, searching for Tyler and Julia. To my relief, I catch sight of them as they board a bus together.

Charlie's gone to meet Jon at the oak and I run to my locker. I rummage through my knapsack and pull out a piece of paper, fold it neatly and slip it into my back pocket.

Dread springs to life as I head outside. Before turning the final corner, that will probably bring me face to face with the school bully, I text Jon. *Almost there. Pls keep an eye on me.* I wait for his reply before taking another step.

The familiar buzz of my phone tells me he's answered. *I see him. He's waiting. I won't let anything happen 2 U. UR my girl.*

If I wasn't so scared, I'd smile.

The sound of rocks ricocheting off a steel utility door alerts me to Nino's presence and his anger.

I plaster on a confident scowl. "You had the guts to show," I yell as I round the corner.

He turns, his knuckles whiten around a large gray rock, and I flinch thinking he's going to whip it at my head. Instead, he throws it a few feet in the air and kicks it out into the field.

"I'm here. What the fuck do you want?" He steps closer, hands fisted at his sides. His flushed face and ropey-veined neck are more evidence of his mood. A twinge of fear shoots through me and I allow it. It's okay to feel right now, I tell myself. It's *good* to feel right now.

"I want to show you something."

"You got nothin' I wanna see." He sneers.

"Don't you want to know more about my secret?"

"Your secret?"

"Yeah, you know what I'm talking about... I can *vanish*." I hate the lame sound of the words as they leave my mouth, because they sound ridiculous. I fight to keep my confident expression in place.

He howls with laughter. "Holy shit. You really are nuts. I thought Jon was just shittin' me. You mean to tell me, you came here to *show* me how you can disappear?" Nino moves to a picnic table and perches on the edge. "You're fat and ugly so disappearin' is probably a good thing... for *everyone*. This oughta be good. Go ahead, pig, disappear."

I flash on the scene at the park where I disappeared the day Nino punched me in the back of the head and wonder why my ability to vanish is so hard for him to fathom. After all, hadn't I already proved it to him? One moment I was there, the next I was gone. I suppose he's just too dense to realize it, or it's too ludicrous a thought to really believe.

Nino's gaze is intense and I'm keenly aware of the fact I'm the center of attention, yet strangely my fear has withered. With closed eyes, I try to conjure up feelings of humiliation and self-hatred. I think of the hurtful words Nino's used to wound me as well as the look of disgust in his eyes, yet still my heart beats evenly, almost serenely. Doesn't it matter what he thinks of me any more? A strange delight creeps its way into me and I have to fight the smile wanting to form on my lips.

"Hurry up, dyke. I wanna go home."

A sharp thud bashes my head and a warm trickle runs from my hairline into my eyes. Pain screams through my skull and I bite my lip to keep from crying out. I finger the sticky wet spot. Blood. He's thrown a rock at me after all.

Quickly, I glance to the oak to make sure Jon and Charlie haven't blown their cover.

I scoop up the egg-sized rock and bounce it in my hand. Rage has found me.

"Don't you fuckin' dare," he says, standing.

My hand is like a catapult ready to spring and he's on me, grabbing my wrist in a vice-like grip. In one fluid movement, my arm's pinned behind me and he's pushing it upwards. Pain tears through me, eliciting a grunt and I fall to my knees. Adrenaline-laced fear trips my heart.

"Jesus Christ!" Nino hollers. He lets go and backs away.

From behind him, Jon and Charlie creep out from their hiding place.

147

Nino backs up against the brick wall of the school and smacks hard against it, losing his footing and hitting the pavement.

I follow him step for step. The word "dyke" wheels around in my brain and I think of what he's planning to do to my best friend. My hands squeeze into fists and I punch him as hard as I can. There's a crunch of cartilage as I connect with his nose. Blood spurts.

"Please. I'm sorry!" he screams, whipping his head around wildly, looking for any sign of me.

I bring my leg back and bash him in the balls. A cry tears from his throat and he slides onto his side cradling his wounded testicles in his hands. Bits of dirt and dried grass stick to his bloodied face.

"He's had enough," Jon calls from behind me.

Unexpected tears, stinging and hot, rise in my eyes. Revenge didn't feel as good as I thought it would.

Nino writhes and moans on the dirty pavement.

I step away, suddenly ashamed and take long slow breaths.

"Time to calm down and come back," Charlie soothes, talking to the air around her.

She spots me when I reappear and is quick to wrap her arms around me. "You did good," she whispers and rocks me back and forth until my heart settles into its normal rhythm.

Jon helps Nino to his feet and onto a picnic table bench, where he sits slumped with his hands wedged between his legs, protecting his tender swollen gonads.

"Freak," Nino snarls and spits a wad of rose-tinged saliva at my feet.

I move toward him. His hands fly protectively to his face and he cowers. But I don't mean to hurt him. I almost want to hug him; to comfort him. I stare down at the swollen red knuckles of my right hand. What have I done?

I've never been so out of control, so desperately violent. "Sorry," I mutter too softly for him to hear and turn away.

He inches to the farthest end of the bench and cautiously lets his hands fall. "You in on this?" he says to Jon, clearing his throat wetly and trying to reclaim some of his bravado with a defiant flick of his hair.

"Damn right." Jon brings his face inches from Nino's. "And this ain't over yet, buddy. You've got more payback comin'."

I want to jump in and say 'no, it's over. It's over right now,' but I keep silent. He can't be let off the hook this easily, not with what he has planned for Charlie.

"What the fuck is she, man?" Fear and disbelief mingle in his expression.

"She's the best thing that ever happened to me." Jon throws an arm around my shoulder. Here's where I should beam but I'm not feeling worthy of such a grandiose claim.

"Give him the speech," Charlie says.

I pull the folded sheet of paper from my pocket and throw it on the table.

"We know what you were planning to do to us," she adds bitterly.

His mouth twists into a crooked smile. "You can't prove shit."

Charlie slams a palm down beside him, making him flinch. "So you admit it? You son of a bitch."

"I don't know what the fuck you're talking about." He's smiling, but I see hot blood pulsing at the side of his neck.

It only takes the gentlest of touches to pull Charlie away. She's only playing at looking fierce.

"This is your new acceptance speech," Jon says. "If you don't read it out loud in front of all the students, teachers and parents at grad, Lola will be your worst nightmare. You won't now when or where but she'll come back to finish what she started. You won't see her coming and the next time, no one will stop her."

Is he talking about me? Jon's words make me sound like a mob henchman.

Nino picks up the sheet. His face crumples in disbelief as he reads. Finally, his eyes flicker from Jon's to mine. "The fuck I will," he says and shreds it into tiny pieces then throws them into the air. They land on my head and shoulders like confetti.

"I've got more copies," I say flatly.

"If you don't do what we say, then she'll have to join you on stage. She'll be right there with you. No one will see her ... who knows what she'll do," Jon says taking my hand and pulling me close.

"What are you gonna do? Beat the shit out of me in front of everyone?" Nino says, eyeing me.

"No," Jon answers, "but she might pull your pants down and give everyone a free show."

Chapter Thirty-One

Final exams were two days ago and graduation is tomorrow. I can't believe how much my confidence has grown in these last few days. But in that there is the danger I won't be able to disappear when I need to. Grandma Rose told me, The Vanishing would stop when I finally loved myself.

Although it's been days since I did what I did to Nino, I still don't like to think about it. Part of me can't really believe I actually beat him up, but a bigger part is ashamed, though I don't tell Jon or Charlie. They ask everyday if I'm still on board with the plan, as if they sense my ambivalence. What choice do I have? I'm in this thing 'til the end. I'm doing it for Charlie.

Today, I go for my first ever manicure and pedicure, and I'm a little nervous, not knowing what to expect and because I'm afraid of turning into *that* type of girl. All those years of watching Eva and Mom making themselves look like strippers, turned me off every kind of female pampering there is. Yet, something has awakened inside me; my inner goddess, I guess. Mom says all women have one. But I think it's Jon who's lit a fire in my heart and helped me realize I *do* want to look my best, but on my own terms.

I've promised to take care of myself because finally, I feel as if I'm worth the effort. The pounds are still melting off and I've even had to have my grad dress taken in and that was a thrill-and-a-half! I snuck away to the mall and bought shoes and actually had fun shoe-shopping all by my lonesome. They're silver/gray spiky heels that tie around the ankle. When I put them on, I've got to be at least six feet tall, but I'll hold my head high and throw my shoulders back, embracing my height. It's me, after all, and if I'm going to love myself, I've gotta love every inch.

Make-up still throws me for a loop and I'm at a loss when it comes to shopping for it. I don't quite trust my own taste and I'm easing my way into the foreign territory of the cosmetics section of the department store, stopping every so often to ask for samples and try the testers. I thought about asking Eva to help me pick some stuff, but instead, I'll ask to borrow her suitcase of make-up. If she says no, I'll pull out Mom's stash. She doesn't have as much, but at least I know she won't mind.

Tomorrow morning I have an appointment at the salon. I can't remember the last time I had my hair styled by a really good hairdresser. I usually go into one of those cheap places at the mall where they don't even wash your hair, just spritz it with a water bottle, give you a quick trim and $15 later, you're out the door, without even a blow dry.

I'm more of a girl than I thought.

Charlie's at the nail salon before me, waiting outside with a large tea and a croissant. "I'm only here to keep you company. I'm not wasting my money on these girly things," she proclaims, shaking her head. "And I never thought you were the type either."

"I suppose it's Jon. He's bringing out my inner diva." I bat my eyelashes exaggeratedly.

She hands me the tea and napkin-wrapped croissant.

"Thanks," I say, surprised they're for me.

Thank goodness the pedicure is first. I doubt I'd be able to eat and drink while getting a manicure. I choose a muted pink polish, pull my pant legs up, exposing my freshly shaven legs and slip my feet into the relaxing warmth of the pulsating water. Embarrassment at this self-indulgence competes with my newfound confidence, but I manage to push the feelings away. I'm not selling out. I'm becoming the me who was always there, under the quiet, rough exterior.

After my pedicure, I get a French manicure. My nails are beautiful in their classy elegance and I want to keep them up. The salon owner tells me to come back in two weeks for a fill and I pretend to know what that means.

"Do you want to get your hair done with me tomorrow morning?" I ask Charlie as we leave the nail salon on our way to her house.

"Naw. I'm good with doin' it myself." She sighs. "You scared?"

"Why would I be scared?"

"You know... about the Nino thing?"

Her question breaks my good mood. I am scared. "A little," I answer.

Nino's avoided me like the plague since the day in the courtyard and that's fine with me. The less I see of him, the better. But we'll be together for the graduation ceremony and when he goes up on stage for his award, I'll have to vanish and trail him to make sure he reads the speech I wrote. Fear begins to creep around in my belly at the thought of what I'll have to do if he doesn't read it. With thumb and forefinger, I give my temples a quick rub to stave off the headache blooming there.

My eyes find Charlie. An unsure smile settles on her lips and her eyebrows arch into a question mark. "You still on board? You can still do the invisible thing, right?"

The last time I vanished was the day in the courtyard with Nino and if he hadn't thrown that rock at me, I'm not sure I would have winked out. I'm fearful my good moods are keeping me grounded, too grounded to disappear.

"Yeah, yeah, don't worry." I hope I sound convincing.

Charlie heaves a sigh. "You're so different now, Lola. You've lost your edge."

I smile. "I know. I feel like a new person."

A frown creases her forehead. "But I like the old Lola."

Her words hit like a jackhammer to the chest. "I'm just trying to better myself. I want to be pretty and lose weight and be accepted." My tone is defensive.

"Listen to what you're saying. You're selling out. I'm not saying you shouldn't look nice, but don't lose yourself in the process. Don't change yourself for a *boy*, or for what you think everyone else's version of pretty is."

"That's not what I'm doing. I really am doing all this for me." I search her eyes for understanding and to make sure she believes me. "It makes me happy to look nice. What's wrong with that?"

We're silent for a moment, then Charlie takes my hand. "Nothing," she says finally. "Just don't leave me behind, okay?"

I give her hand a squeeze. "I love you, Charlie. I *really* do. You're my best friend and I will never *ever* leave you behind."

A smile sweeps across her face and tears well in her eyes. She pulls me into her arms and holds tight. Time slowly passes, measured by the beating of our hearts. Then her lips meet mine in a soft, sweet lingering kiss.

She pulls away. "Oh, my God, Lola, I'm sorry, I didn't mean to…" Her eyes are wide, searching my expression, looking for something… but what? Anger? Shock? *Desire*?

Charlie backs away, eyes still glued to mine. Then she turns and bolts up her front steps, leaving me on the sidewalk in front of her house. The door slams shut behind her.

My walk home is one of dazed confusion and fear. I'm afraid that what's just happened will change things between us forever. Embarrassment and a peculiar sensation in the pit of my stomach follow me like a guilty conscience.

When I get home, Jon's waiting on the front steps of my house. He stands as I approach, and a broad grin spans the width of his face.

"Hi. I rang the bell and no one was home, so I thought I'd wait. Hope that's okay and not creepy," he says.

I can't help it. I jump into his arms, nearly sending the two of us backwards into the rose bushes.

"Whoa, what's going on?" he asks into my hair as I hug him to me.

"Nothing. I'm just glad you're here."

"I'm glad I am too." He holds me at arm's length. "Are you sure you're okay? Is it tomorrow? Are you freaked out about it?"

I nod vigorously. "Yeah, that's it. I'm nervous about grad and the Nino thing." I pull him by the hand up the front steps and into the house.

I make us a cup of tea, even though the last thing I want is another one since downing the extra large orange pekoe Charlie brought me. My bladder is near exploding. I excuse myself and run to the bathroom.

When I get back to the kitchen, I'm tempted to tell Jon what happened with Charlie, but loyalty to my friend prevents it. I don't think Charlie would want him to know. It's kinda like she just hit on his girlfriend and might make things weird between them. But there's nothing that can take away the weirdness that's now hanging between Charlie and me. How am I going to face her at graduation tomorrow?

An odd mix of emotions run through me. Charlie's kiss was tender and sweet and strangely exciting. For a moment, I consider I just might be a lesbian, after all, but the thought passes when I remember the power of Jon's kisses – his make me dizzy and knock me off my feet.

"Where are your parents and sister?" Jon asks.

"Not home."

He throws me a mischievous smile, an eyebrow arches and he slowly rises.

For the second time in less than an hour, I'm kissed. I throw my arms around the boy I love and kiss him back in closed-eyed ecstasy.

Chapter Thirty-Two

Butterflies rumble uncomfortably, and cramps knife my stomach, sending waves of nausea through me. It's the morning of graduation and the way I see it, there are only two ways this day can end, with the humiliation of failure, or with sweet revenge. From a place higher than myself, maybe even from God, I get the distinct feeling that whatever this day brings, it will set the tone for the rest of my life. This day will be epic!

Eva's in the bathroom. I knock softly on the door and she yanks it open, a toothbrush sticks out of her Colgate-foamed mouth.

"What do you want?" Her words are garbled.

"Will you help me today?" I ask with hesitation.

She spits and rinses, then replaces her toothbrush it in its holder. "With what?"

"Getting ready for graduation?"

She studies me for a moment then shrugs. "Why not? When do you need me?"

Secretly, I don't think Eva can resist an opportunity for a makeover. She lives for them. "I've got a hair appointment at 10:30, the ceremony is at 1:30, but the dance is at night, so could you help me get ready for the dance?"

"Okay. Come get me when you need me."

"Thanks." Relief fills me. That was easier than I thought.

Eva gives me a flicker of a smile and steps out of the bathroom. I move forward to enter and she stops me with a light touch on the hand. "You look good lately, Lola. You've lost a bit of weight."

I beam. "Really? You can tell?"

"Yeah, sure, but you've still got a long way to go." She continues on her way and my smile goes out. After all the times Eva's been mean to me, you'd think I would have learned my lesson by now, but I fall into her trap every time. Something in me wants to believe there's good in her and that there's hope for us, as sisters.

After brushing my teeth and dressing, I head to the kitchen.

Mom's at the table with her coffee. "Are you excited?" she asks.

"A little," I say as I fill a bowl with cereal and milk and sit.

"Dad will be home early today. He had a couple of things to take care of at the shop." She wraps her hands around her mug and smiles, eyes trained on me. "This is it, Lola, honey. You're off to university in September. I can't believe it. You know you'll be the first in the family to go." Now her hands are clasped together in front of her chest and she looks like she's praying. "Have you decided on a major?"

I'd been trying not to have this conversation. Mom knows about my aspirations, but I think she's convinced herself I'm going to change my mind once I actually get to university. If I tell her I've decided to major in English so I can be a writer, she'll think it's a waste of time and money. Neither of my parents graduated high school and though hard working, their blue collar backgrounds have given them a practical, feet firmly planted on the ground approach to life. They don't think in terms of careers, only jobs and a great future to them is if I snag an office job at a company with benefits and a pension.

Dad's an auto mechanic and Mom used to work at the nail salon until things got slow. Now she's a cashier at No Frills. But deep inside her lurks the soul of an artist. I've witnessed it. As a matter of fact, I see it each and every day right on her face. To Mom, make-up is paint and her face is the canvas. A sudden inspiration sneaks up on me.

"Mom, you know how you tell me all the time you wished you hadn't dropped out of beauty school?"

She nods. "Yeah."

"Why is that?"

She sips her coffee and purses her lips thoughtfully. "I guess it's because I really loved making women look the best they could."

"So, you liked to bring out their best qualities?"

"I guess."

"And how did you do that?"

"Lola, what's with all the questions all of a sudden?"

I heave a sigh. "Just answer me."

She throws up her hands. "Okay, okay. Just don't know what you're getting at." She stares off into the distance, as if tugging at the memories, trying to pull them into her mind. "I really loved making their eyes beautiful," she says finally. "I think eye make-up, if done well, is the most important thing a woman can do to enhance her looks. That and hair extensions, of course."

I try not to roll my eyes at the mention of hair extensions. "And when you did their eye make-up, was it similar to painting a portrait? I mean, with all the mixing and blending of the eye shadows? Knowing where to put what color?"

Her eyes shine and her face breaks into a huge smile. "Yes, that's a great way to put it, Lola. You've pegged it."

Bingo! Eva's not the only one good at setting traps in this family. "That feeling is the creative energy in you coming to the surface. I think it comes straight from God, into our souls and we bring it into the world for others to appreciate. We all have that potential. I know Grandma Rose had it."

Mom inserts a long-nailed pointer finger into her mop of hair and scratches her head. "You've put a lot of thought into this. I'm not so sure it's all that complicated.

Besides what does all of this have to do with your major?" She's eyeing me suspiciously now.

"I'm going to major in English so I can be a writer," I say confidently. "Because writing is what makes me feel the way you did, when you were in beauty school doing makeovers. It's my creative outlet and it's what my soul wants to do."

"Oh," she says, disappointment in her voice, eyebrows arching toward her hairline. "Yes, you did mention that before, only..."

"Only what?" I say flatly. God, is she that dense that she can't see the parallels between us? I'm trying to connect. I'm trying to make her understand.

She sighs. "Only I thought you'd have given up on that idea by now. Really, Lola, what kind of a living can you make as a writer? You'll end up in an office job eventually and it'll be a waste of an education."

A fire springs up in me, and all the years of not being heard and not wanting to be seen or noticed are shed. I stand and fix her with a stare. "Writing is my talent, Mom. It's the only thing I know how to do and more importantly, it's what makes me happy. Don't you want me to be happy?" I stomp away, not waiting for an answer and take my bowl of cereal to my room.

A moment later, there's a knock and Mom pushes my door open. "Can I come in?"

I put my bowl down on my night table and fold my arms tightly across my chest. "I don't care," I say with defiant anger.

She curls her feet up under her at the foot of my bed and gives her head a little tilt. Her mass of unruly curls tumble over her forehead, giving her a childlike appearance. "I know we're different, you and I. I try to understand you, and I worry that I never will. But no matter what, you're my daughter and I love you. I do want you to be happy, but I don't think I realized until right now, until

160

you told me in the way you did, just how much you want to be a writer. I want for you what you want for yourself."

My angry resolve melts and I let my arms fall lax, hands settling in my lap. "Really?"

"Really."

I'm shocked but I'm beginning to learn that all it takes to make people understand you is to tell them what you're thinking and feeling. Running from your feelings and keeping things to yourself only creates more distance. It hits me in that moment, what Grandma Rose meant about letting people see me. If I can accept myself for who I am, then others will too.

I inch closer and lean into my mother's arms. "I've waited so long to hear you say you accept me exactly the way I am," I whisper.

"I'm so sorry, honey. I should have taken you seriously the first time you told me you wanted to be a writer. I shouldn't ever have expected you to be a carbon copy of me." She pulls away. Tears stand in her eyes. "Look at me. I know what I am. I'm a middle-aged woman trying to hang onto her youth. My looks were the only thing I ever had. I never had brains like you. I could never make something of myself like I know you will. Yeah, I suppose my dream of being a cosmetician was my creative outlet, and you know what?"

"What?"

"I should never have let that dream slip away." She caresses my cheek and sniffs back tears. "I don't want you to have regrets like I do."

Chapter Thirty-Three

The hairdresser left my curls, like I'd asked. They're me. My thick, dark locks billow out from under my graduation cap and I run a hand through them. Good hair runs in the family. I guess that's something to be thankful for. Lately, I'm finding more and more to love and appreciate about myself, and with that has come a sense of weightiness. Not like a physical heaviness, more like a feeling of being grounded. I'm more present, more here, and more alive, like I've actually got a future to look forward to.

After arriving with our families, we graduates are ushered into the cafeteria where we put on our gowns and caps. Jon and I are only able to spend a few moments together until we're arranged into a line, alphabetically by last name.

"You haven't lost your nerve, have you?" he whispers. His eyes narrow as if he's studying me.

"No," I answer, willing myself to meet his gaze.

"Got your copy of his speech?"

I pat my back pocket where one is tucked away.

"Good girl. Make that asshole pay!" Jon's voice holds a touch of acid.

A bad feeling begins to ferment in the pit of my stomach and I open my mouth to speak, to test the waters with a protest, but he's talking again, "Hey, what's up with Charlie? She's acting all… weird."

We're forced apart and ushered into line. With a shrug I mouth, "Don't know," and hope he can't see the lie in my eyes.

I'm an "S" and he's a "K", so we're too far apart to speak. Charlie's kept her distance. Every time I look at her, she turns away and when I walked up to her earlier, she brushed me off and found somewhere else to be. Guess she's happy her last name's Menardi, only five letters apart but it amounts to too many people between us to be able to chat.

Nino's at the beginning of the line, acting all cocky with his friends. Everyone knows he's a shoe in for the athletic scholarship award, and they're treating him like he's already won it, with slaps on the back and mussing of hair. It's one of the biggest deals in school with the largest scholarship. He glances my way – is that fear in his eyes? His cocky smile goes out as quickly as a candle in a windstorm and he whips his head back around. Someone fearing me feels awkward and wrong. It's true that Eva's a little scared of me, but that's different. She's my sister and despite sometimes hating her, deep down inside I guess I love her. When I beat the crap out of Nino, it only made me feel mean.

"Okay, people, settle down." Mr. Hollingsworth, the head of the science department, yells in his baritone voice over the shouts of four-hundred-and-twenty excited teenagers. "One minute to show time." The decibel level in the room declines noticeably. Mr. Hollingsworth is a no-nonsense kinda guy and is always the heavy in situations like this.

We ready ourselves for our entrance – straighten our caps, make sure the tassel is on the proper side and smooth our gowns. Mr. Hollingsworth herds us into the hallway and lines us up outside the gymnasium. Our families are already settled in the gym. The muffled voices of excited family members and the clang of the school band tuning up can be heard through the heavy metal doors.

The doors swing wide, the band plays and off we march. There's a swell of applause and though I'm excited to soon be a high school graduate, I've got bigger things on my mind.

We follow Mr. Hollingsworth to a section reserved just for us where a program, setting out the itinerary for the ceremony, lies on each chair. I leaf through, searching for the athletic scholarship. It's one of the first awards to be handed out and a small wave of relief fills me; at least I won't have to be nervous for the entire ceremony. I just want to get it over with.

Principal Harris takes the podium. "Welcome, graduates, family, friends and faculty to Maple Ridge Secondary School's 2011 Commencement Ceremony. Before we begin, I'd like to take this opportunity to say a little something to our class of 2011." He's a small, slight man in his late fifties with a close-cropped horseshoe of gray fringe. Why he doesn't just shave off that pitiful little bit of hair is beyond me.

He clears his throat and pulls a small index card from the pocket of his suit jacket. "I hope your dreams take you to the corners of your smiles, to the highest of your hopes, to the windows of your opportunities, and to the most special places your heart has ever known. We are here today to…"

Principal Harris drones on and nothing more sinks into my preoccupied brain. I'm thinking about when Nino's name is called for his award, and how I'll have to duck out and quickly vanish so I can follow him to the podium. I've got a mental list of things I can call up to help me disappear, from the anger and humiliation of the attack at the park, to the heinous acts Nino had planned for Charlie and me.

To help settle my nerves, I pat the speech through my gown. It's still there, but will soon be invisible just like the rest of me. When it leaves my hand and is on the podium in front of Nino, somehow, in some magical way, it'll be back in the visible realm, staring up at Nino, waiting to be read. If he won't read it, and that's what I'm betting on, then I'll throw the gown over his head and yank down his pants, underwear and all. He'll look crazy; like he's just stripped naked in front of the entire graduating class, teachers and parents. Nino Campese will know the agony of embarrassment. The same agony I've felt for years. The agony that has made me feel insignificant and has fostered my desire to be invisible.

A twinge of conscience troubles me. Do I really want another person to feel that way, even if it is Nino?

The polite applause filling the room tells me Principal Harris' speech is over and I snap to attention when he and Vice Principal Bevalaqua begin to call our names.

Diplomas are doled out, accompanied by a quick handshake and a photo op. Family members are told to hold their applause until all the diplomas have been handed out. My turn comes and goes and in less than a minute I'm back in my seat. Danny Zuppatto is last and when he leaves the stage, cheers and hearty accolades ring in my ears.

We're all back in our seats now, gripping the fruit of four years of labor – a rolled up scroll tied with a red silk ribbon. Somehow, it doesn't seem enough. However, I'm officially a high school graduate and I allow a little pride to rush through me. But this day isn't just about graduating high school, it's about an act of forced contrition.

My stomach knots when I think of what's next on the agenda – the award recipients are about to be announced, followed by the Valedictorian address. That ought to be good and boring since the Valedictorian is Ronnie Smithers, a kid more picked on than even me or Charlie. He's thirteen, but since he's a genius, he skipped a bunch of grades. Poor Ronnie. He should be proud, but he's probably scared shitless right now. He never speaks above a whisper and now he's got to make a whole speech and a long one at that. Bet he's wishing he could make himself invisible right about now.

It strikes me that I have nothing prepared on the off-chance I win the writing award. I close my eyes and try to come up with something, but the banging of my heart against my ribcage is too distracting and not a single coherent thought pops to mind. I let the notion slip away with a little sigh of relief. It's easier if I tell myself I'm not going to win.

Jon turns and looks at me. We're too far apart to speak, but his eyes say it all. "Don't wimp out," he's saying, "you've got to do this. Don't let us down." Sucking in a few deep breaths, I drum my fingers on my knee. The girl next to me shoots me a dirty look. It's Patricia Seaver, the pretty cheerleader I sat beside all year in homeroom. She gives me a *tsk* to go with the look, making me want to stomp on her dainty little foot.

One after another, students are called to the stage. Principal Harris congratulates each with a handshake and the student proceeds to the podium to say a few words. Finally, the next award is the athletic scholarship. Adrenaline shoots through me, sending my heart into summersaults. I quickly look at the students on either side of me and study their expressions. No shrieks of surprise or slack jawed stares, so I guess I'm still visible.

I ready myself for a quick escape.

Principal Harris plucks an envelope from the stack in the Vice Principal's outstretched hand. His bald pate gleams in the overhead lights and he pastes on a big, phony smile. "The next award is the athletic scholarship award, male. The winner of this award has shown proven leadership abilities as well as outstanding athletic talent in several intramural sports." He holds the envelope up to the audience before slipping a finger beneath the seal and popping it open. "And the winner is …"

I'm already an inch out of my seat when he calls the *wrong* name.

"… Paul Chang."

I fall back with an audible sigh. Nino's shaking his head and I read his lips. He's spewing a stream of expletives as he pounds his thigh with a fist.

Jon throws his hands up in resignation and meets my gaze with a concerned furrowing of the brow. Charlie hasn't turned to look at me.

He's going to get away without being punished, I think. At first, I'm alarmed, furious even, but I have to admit, a small part of me is relieved. Then I think of Charlie and what he wanted to do to her. There's got to be another way! Maybe Jon and I can come up with something to spring on him at the dance. My eyes burn into the back of Charlie's head, willing her to turn around. God, I need my friend right now.

Paul Chang rushes to the stage, takes his award and hoists it over his head to great applause. He looks as shocked as Nino. After Paul's impromptu ten-second thank you speech, Principal Harris continues, announcing one award after another.

"...and the winner of the creative writing scholarship award is... Lola Savullo."

I snap to attention at the sound of my name. All eyes have turned to me. A smile finally forms on my lips at the realization of what I've just accomplished.

Standing, I make my way to the stage on elastic legs, searching for my parents and Eva in the crowd. Their beaming faces and frantic clapping greet me. They're genuinely happy. Why does that surprise me? I peer down at the rose indelibly etched on the skin of my wrist and run a finger lightly over it, silently thanking Gran for being my inspiration, and my biggest supporter.

"Congratulations, Miss Savullo," Principal Harris says with a handshake as he gives me the award and the scholarship check that comes with it.

A camera flashes. It's Mom. She's rushed to the stage and is now waving wildly up at me.

"Thanks," I manage in a fog of disbelief.

The podium seems as if it's a mile away as I move toward it on trembling legs. When I get there and open my mouth to speak, nothing comes out. What if I just squeak out a thank you and run off? My heart's beating dangerously hard and I fear I'm entering my own personal Bermuda Triangle. There will be no disappearing in front of a gymnasium full of people, I tell myself. Winking out in public wouldn't do much for my freaky, fat girl, possible lesbian reputation.

Nonchalantly, I suck in calming breaths as I search my brain for something, anything to say. I've just won the writing award, surely I can think of something profound. Isn't that what's expected of me, a writer?

I tap the award against the wooden podium. It's rolled up like my diploma and fastened with a dark blue ribbon. The noise it makes is a hollow *pong*, like the sound of an empty paper towel roll. My other hand grips the envelope containing my scholarship check. When I realize I'm crinkling it, I relax my grip.

The room is silent, except for the *pong, pong* of my rolled up award and the glare of expectant eyes brings heat to my cheeks. Jon's staring at me so hard it's as if he's willing my mouth to move; by shear force of will, he's trying to pull words from me. Charlie's in the row behind Jon and she's smiling. I hope it's for my success and not my failure at public speaking.

My gaze falls on Nino. His dark eyes are heavy-lidded with pleasure and his lips are curled into a satisfied grin. Despite whatever fear I'd managed to strike in him earlier, he's clearly enjoying my giant fail.

As soon as our eyes meet, he speaks, "Cows can't talk. Say moo, cow." It isn't loud, but he's near enough for me to hear.

Pride fades and self-hatred and humiliation rise up to take its place. Those feelings are familiar; they are my default. The warmth of tears spring to my eyes, but I pinch them away. Grandma Rose's sweet face flashes across the screen of my mind and, absently, I caress my tattoo. "You must learn to love yourself." Her words echo in my ears and are as real as if she were standing by my side whispering them, like the day I wrote my story.

I gather up the back of my gown and pull Nino's speech from my pocket, unfold it and iron it flat with the palm of my hand.

Emboldened, I face the audience and clear my throat. "This speech was meant for someone else to read, but I think it needs to be heard," I say. But do I really mean it? Or am I doing this because I feel I have to?

Nino's eyes are wide and he leans forward as if he can't believe I'm going to do it. I notice a slight discoloration on his left cheek. The purple and yellow of a faded bruise? Did I do that? My gaze falls to the small cut that still lingers on my hand from the day I punched him. Red-ringed, but fading, nevertheless it's a reminder. I glance over at my fellow graduates. They know Nino. Everyone knows Nino, teachers and students alike. I won't be telling them anything they don't already know, except for the cruel plans he had for Charlie and me after the dance tonight. And maybe no one will believe me. Like Nino said, I can't prove shit.

My splayed fingers gather the sheet up slowly and I hear it crumple as my hand clenches into a fist, then I toss it to the floor. I have a choice. Become a bully, like Nino and read the speech, with its biting angry words that will humiliate him and perpetuate this ugliness, or I can rise above and use my time to say something that really matters.

Principal Harris inches his way toward me and I realize I'd better say something or I'll be kicked back to my seat. I must look like a fool standing so quietly at the podium.

I suck in a deep breath and begin, "I wouldn't want to be anybody else." My voice is strong and sure. "I used to want to be anybody but me, but right now I realize that if I wasn't Lola Savullo, all five foot nine inches of me, with this wild curly hair and my love of reading and writing, I wouldn't be standing here right now enjoying the proudest moment of my life."

"Yeah, all four hundred pounds of you," Nino yells loud enough for most everyone to hear.

He draws sharp warning glares from teachers. Principal Harris and Vice Principal Bevelaqua both shoot him narrow-eyed admonitions. There's a gasp and a few low boos from the audience. Just weeks ago that comment would have set me off, melting what little self-esteem I had. It would have sent my heart into a flutter and I more than likely would have disappeared. But not any more.

I straighten to my full height as I peer down at Nino, who's slouched in his chair, arms folded across his chest with a smirk on his face.

Principal Harris has moved close again. "It's okay," I say and hold up a hand, my left hand, the one with my beautiful rose. I look pointedly at Nino and speak just to him, "I'm the one standing here. I'm the one who won a scholarship for my talent. I'm the one who's going to make something of myself."

Nino's smirk dissolves and a calm unlike anything I've ever experienced washes over me, as if I'm enfolded in the warmth of an embrace. Grandma Rose, maybe? I can't be certain but it's a comforting thought.

I turn toward the teachers. "Thank you for the award and the scholarship. I will use it to help make my dreams come true." Then I face the crowd. "Thanks to my dearest and best friend, Charlie Menardi, who believes in me and has stood by my side through thick and thin. I will be there for you always and forever." For a moment, it's as if we're the only ones in the room. Her expression softens and a flicker of a smile plays on her lips.

Then my eyes find Jon. "Thank you to Jon Kingsbury. My dear sweet friend who wants nothing more than to protect me." His scowl, no doubt at the failure of our plan, turns to a smile.

Next, I search out my family. "Thank you to my parents and even my sister, Eva, for giving me lots of material to write about." The crowd laughs and thankfully my family does too.

"And thank you." I point at Nino and at Tyler. "For showing me what I'm made of. For helping me discover a strength I never thought I possessed and for showing me that I don't want to be cruel. That I don't want revenge and that being a bully is something to be pitied, not rewarded." My voice is soft and conversational because these words are not meant to hurt or humiliate. They're meant for me. It feels good to speak my truth. This isn't revenge, it's me honoring my self-worth.

My gaze shifts to the sky. "But most of all, thank you, Grandma Rose, for loving me and teaching me how important it is for me to love myself." My voice catches as I fight back tears and I step away from the podium. "Can you see me, Grandma?" I whisper as I trace the outline of my rose.

Charlie's on her feet and to my delight she makes her way to the stage and stands beside me, wrapping an arm around my waist. I pull her close.

"Are we friends?" I ask.

She nods and when she does, tears fall, leaving tiny darkened polka dots on her navy gown. Together we make our way back to our seats.

Nino huffs his displeasure but I can hardly hear it over the applause my speech has brought.

Chapter Thirty-Four

Ronnie Smithers' Valedictorian speech, filled with stutters and stammers, comes to an end and his freckled face flushes to the same orangey-red as his ginger-topped head. The gym fills with polite applause and Mr. Hollingsworth is quickly on his feet, perhaps as a diversion to deflect attention from the petrified boy. He gestures wildly for us to stand too. We do and then someone throws their cap in the air like they do in the movies. A split second later, it's as if we all share one brain because we're all throwing our caps almost at the same time.

Principal Harris announces that the ceremony is now over and there's coffee and pastries set out at the far end of the gym. Chairs scrape and suddenly there's a loud buzz of conversation as everyone makes their way to the refreshment table.

After retrieving *a* cap, because I can't be certain it's the same one I'd been wearing, I make my way over to the rear of the gym.

I spy Mom searching the crowd for me. Despite the extra three-and-a-half inches her spiky heels have given her, she's still pretty much shorter than everyone around her. It's the bobbing of her multi-colored head of hair that I spot first. My sister's snagged a pile of Danishes and she's folding them up in a napkin. Dad's holding a coffee, no doubt wishing he had a cigarette to go with it, and talking to Charlie's mom.

As soon as Mom sees me, she pulls me into an embrace. "Oh, my God, Lola. You won an award!"

"Yup," I say. "Can we go now? I want to get ready for the dance?" Truth be told, I just want to get outside for some air.

Although I'm happy and proud of myself, my emotions are raw. And Nino and Tyler are floating around amongst the crowd somewhere and I'd rather not see them right now.

"In a minute." She pats my arm and joins in on Dad's conversation.

"Hey," Charlie says as she reaches through the crowd and grabs a small square of lemon cake. "Congrats. I knew you'd win." She points toward my award with the cake-toting hand.

"Thanks. I didn't."

There's an awkward silence. I guess we're both thinking about what happened between us the other day. My gaze drops to my shoes.

"You excited about the dance?" she asks quickly in a voice higher than her usual tone.

The question draws my attention back to her. "Umm, yeah, I guess."

"Me too," she says, reaching tentatively for my hand. "Who woulda thought we'd be happy about going to a dance?" She laughs, and then leans in as if to reveal a secret. "Thank you for the nice things you said about me."

The crazy awkwardness slides away and I smile with relief. "Meant every word."

Charlie widens her eyes and blows out her cheeks. "So, I guess Nino got away with it." She eats her tiny piece of cake in one bite.

I shake my head with vigor. "He didn't get away with anything."

"Sure he did. He didn't win the award so he didn't have to read the speech you wrote for him. Then when you won, I thought you were going to read it." There's surprise in her voice and a question in her expression.

I play with the tassel on my cap, then finally plant the odd square hat on my head. Charlie knows what it's like to be bullied, just as well as I do, but only I know what being the bully feels like. "Would you like to be him?" I ask.

"What?" Confusion furrows her brow.

"Would you like to be Nino?" I say again. "Because I know what it feels like to be a bully. When I punched him and kicked him in the nuts the other day, I hated myself for doing that."

"What? It didn't feel good to beat the shit out of him?" Her mouth hangs open like a gate on a busted hinge.

"It felt awful and I don't ever want to feel that way again." I plant my hands on my hips.

She raises her hands in a gesture of surrender. "I didn't think about it like that."

"All you and Jon wanted was revenge and I was the big dog you two sent in after the bully." I'm careful to keep my voice even. We've just gotten over one awkward moment and the last thing I want is another.

"I'm sorry, Lola. I didn't know…"

"It's okay," I take a deep breath and let it out slowly. "It's over now. Can we just let it all go?"

"Sure, sure." She puts a hand on my arm and nods furiously.

My cellphone vibrates. I gather up my gown and slide it from my pocket. *At the doors with parents and grandparents. Can't get away.*

"It's Jon," I say and turn in a circle until I spot him. A huge smile splits his face when our eyes meet and despite the tiny temper tantrum I've just thrown, I smile back.

It's ok. See u at the dance, I text back.

He reads it and waves. Then he blows me a kiss.

"Jon's by the doors. He can't get away," I explain.

"Are you mad at him too?" Charlie asks.

"No. I'm not mad at anyone," I answer without hesitation. "And that's the greatest part, Char'. I'm not mad, I'm happy."

"Then so am I."

Chapter Thirty-Five

Relief floods through me as I slide into the backseat of our SUV. All the hard stuff is over and I can relax now and have fun at the dance. A few short weeks ago, I'd be in hell at the prospect of being dressed up, and of course I'd be dateless. Life has a way of changing when you least expect it – for good and for bad.

"Way to go, Lola," Dad says as we drive away. "Congratulations for being a high school graduate and for winning an award. How much is the check for?"

Mom plants a hand on Dad's arm and shoots him a look, then she turns in her seat to face me. "Lola, what was going on with that boy? What did he say to you?"

I glimpse Dad's smile melt in the rear view. Phew, I almost want to say out loud. Guess they didn't hear what Nino said and I'm glad for it. "Ahh, nothing important."

"Was he making fun of you?" she tries again. Her face crumples in concern.

"I'm happy right now. I just wanna let the good feelings in and be proud. It doesn't matter what that loser said."

"That's the attitude," Dad chimes in.

"Has this been going on for a while?" Mom's nothing if not persistent.

"High school's full of buttheads," Eva chimes in. "God, Mom, this kinda crap goes on all the time. I remember when I was in my junior year, there was this one girl…" Mom waves her quiet and keeps her eyes on me.

"I'm sorry, honey." She reaches out to me and I take her hand.

"It's really okay." I give her tiny hand a squeeze. It's in her eyes – she knows this wasn't a one-time thing. It's as if right in this moment she's seeing me the way the kids in school do. I want to roll into a ball and hide.

Her lips twitch into an unsure smile. "I'm proud of what you said. You gave that boy a dressing down; put him in his place." Her smile goes out and is replaced by a thin grim line as if a sudden worry has struck her. "Maybe you shouldn't go to the dance tonight. Is this boy... dangerous?"

My heart takes off in a sprint. "I have a date!" I almost scream. "It's my first date ever, Mom. You can't do this to me." I look to Dad for back-up, my eyes pleading.

"She's right, honey," Dad says. "We can't spoil her night."

Mom's quiet for a moment. Finally, her expression relaxes and she heaves a sigh. "Okay," she says to Dad, then turns to me. "You deserve to have some fun. Besides, you've got that great dress waiting for you."

There's more of Grandma Rose in her than I'd expected. Or maybe it's that I never really noticed before.

"Thanks," I reply. "And, no, he's not dangerous," I lie. If they knew the whole story – how Nino had bullied me all through high school, how he'd punched me and was planning to give me a really good beating this very evening. And the unspeakable deed he had planned for Charlie. If they knew all that, I'd never be allowed out of the house again. Dad would call the cops and this craziness would escalate.

Nino's not going to hurt me or Charlie now. Having his plans revealed I suppose has something to do with it. But there's something more. It's like in the Wizard of Oz when Dorothy sees the wizard and he's not so scary or powerful, after all. That's how it is for me now with Nino. I've seen him cry, hell, I've *made* him cry and although I'm ashamed of what I did, I think it's good that he's scared of me.

* * * *

Once home, I grab a snack and head upstairs to get ready.

"Hey, thought you wanted my help," Eva calls after me.

"I do." I'm surprised she remembered.

"Okay, then go to my room."

I sit at Eva's make-up table and eye myself in the mirror, while she cracks open her suitcase of cosmetics. My hair's held up, thankfully. It's still full and curly. Arching a brow, I smile at my reflection. My teeth have always been straight and white thanks to a full year of braces in grade nine, and whitening strips. They were my only indulgence in four years of high school. My face is taking on a more angular look; cheek-bones are slowly emerging.

"Close your eyes," Eva commands.

She dabs on cream and then foundation and smoothes it over my face. "What color did you say your dress was?"

"Black."

"Okay, let's go for a smoky eye. Keep your eyes closed."

My lids are brushed, my lashes curled, then mascara is applied. My cheeks are bronzed and finally my lips are lined, then swiped with whatever color Eva deems appropriate. I'm afraid I'm going to look like a hooker or, at best, a pole dancer.

After what feels like an eternity, she finally says, "Okay, you can look now."

"I'm beautiful," I whisper, hardly believing the woman staring back from the mirror is me.

Eva beams.

"Thank you so much," I say.

"You're welcome." She takes my hand. "You know, you really are... *beautiful*, I mean," she says softly, a smile unfurling across her face.

I sit in stunned silence, waiting for the zinger that always follows one of Eva's compliments, but it doesn't come. After a pause of a few beats, I risk my heart and allow it to open a crack. "Thank you, that really means a lot to me."

She looks away as if the show of emotion makes her uncomfortable. We're so used to fighting, arguing and bickering; kindness is foreign and uncomfortable.

"And I'm sorry," she adds.

"For what?"

"I've been mean. I don't want to hurt you any more."

Her eyes mist over. I have to fight my own tears from ruining Eva's work.

"It's okay. I'm mean to you too sometimes. I think that's how sisters are. I just don't think you and I understand each other. But I want more than anything for us to be friends."

She pulls me into an embrace. "We will. I promise. From now on, Lola, you and me will be the best of friends."

Just when I thought this day could get no better, it has. Right now, things are a little weird and unfamiliar, but I silently vow to not only *be* a friend to my sister, but to *let* her be a friend to me.

"Let me get my dress on. Be right back," I announce excitedly.

I run to my room and slip into my dress, put on my heels and jewelry, then make my way back. When I push open the door, Mom, Dad and Eva are waiting and I enter to catcalls and applause.

Chapter Thirty-Six

Dad drops me off at the banquet hall for the dance.

"Call if you need me and don't hesitate to tell a teacher if that kid comes near you?" he says through the rolled down passenger-side window.

"Okay." I wave and turn to walk away.

"Is he here? Do you see him?"

I turn back around and shrug. "Don't know yet, Dad." Impatience edges my voice.

He rubs his stubbly chin then sighs. "Okay, go on. Have a great night."

I make my way around to the driver's side window and kiss his cheek.

"Thank you, Daddy."

He cups a hand under my chin. "Love you, my Lola."

"I love you too," I whisper and finally walk away.

A few kids are milling around outside, taking pictures and laughing. I wave to Dad when I get to the front door. But he doesn't leave just yet. I guess he's going to hang around for a little while.

The banquet hall is done up in black and silver. Balloons and flowers are everywhere. Cameras flash as I walk into the din of conversation surrounding me. The D.J. is set up and music throbs, giving the room a party atmosphere.

"Wow," a voice says from behind and I spin around to find Jon. He's handsome in his dark gray suit and black and silver tie. His hair's shorter and is slicked to standing on the top of his head in a faux Mohawk. I loved his wavy long hair but he looks older, more mature, like the college student he'll soon be.

"You look gorgeous." He smiles a big goofy grin and gives me the once-over.

Blushing furiously, I look around at anything but him. "You look pretty cute yourself. I like the hair cut," I manage to say. The heat of embarrassment warms my chest and neck.

"Aw, shucks." He kicks at the floor like a ten-year-old. Jon takes my hands and his expression turns serious. "Tell me you're mine, Lola."

He leans close and I'm intoxicated by the smell of him. I put my arms around his neck and kiss him softly. "I'm yours," I whisper.

The kiss is long and lingering, but when he pulls away, he says, "It's okay, you know."

My eyes widen. "What's okay?"

"That we didn't get Nino. Don't get me wrong, I still hate the guy, but I think it all ended perfectly. He didn't win a scholarship and you did. This time, the good guy won."

My heart melts and I pull him to me again.

"Knock if off, you two," Charlie says. I turn to find her with her date.

"This is Robin," she says.

I hold out a hand in greeting. "Charlie's kept you a secret. It's nice to finally meet you."

"We met at work," Robin replies.

Robin's fair with red shoulder-length hair and her pale blue eyes shine even in the dimly lit room.

"Your dress is really pretty," I say.

"Thanks, Charlie helped me pick it out."

"I can't imagine Charlie picking out anything like *that*," I reply.

Robin laughs. "She's actually got good taste." She smiles at Charlie who's dressed in black skinny jeans and sneakers, a shiny silver dinner jacket complete with a black dress shirt and a narrow tie, pulled askew at the neck.

"I picked you, didn't I?" Charlie says with a wink. She throws an arm around Robin's shoulders and plants a kiss her on the cheek. "I'll be right back, okay? I just need to talk to Lola for a sec."

Robin nods.

I eye Jon and get an approving smile.

Charlie leads me to a table at the other end of the room. "Have a seat." She pulls out a chair for me and one for her. "You look really nice, by the way."

"Thanks. And you... well, you look like Charlie. The Charlie I've missed, even though it's only been a day." I regard her for a moment. "We're okay now, right?"

"Yes, of course. I'm really *really* sorry, Lola. I shouldn't have..."

"It's okay. It was kinda flattering." I smile and she looks away shyly.

"How do you like Robin?"

"She's pretty and she seems nice. Are you happy?"

Charlie takes a deep breath. "I think I can be happy with Robin, *eventually*. I mean, everything's so new right now. How about you, are you happy?"

"Never better." I beam.

"I'm so proud of you – for winning and for what you said up there."

"Thanks."

She leans closer. "Have you noticed?"

"Noticed what?"

"You can't feel it?"

A smile sweeps across my face. "What are you talking about?"

"Look around you. Everyone is talking about you. Lola Savullo, the girl who put Nino Campese and Tyler Campbell in their place."

I sneak a furtive glace around. She's right. Eyes *are* on me and when my gaze meets another, there are smiles and nods. So very different from what I'm used to. It feels so damn good to finally be seen.

"Do you think Nino and Tyler will show up tonight?"

Charlie shrugs. "Hope not. I don't want to be self-conscious about bringing a girl."

"You know what I've learned over this last little while?"

Charlie shakes her head.

"I've learned that it doesn't matter what anyone thinks about you, what nasty things they say or do. The only thing that matters is whether or not you *choose* to believe them." I stand and pull Charlie to her feet. "Hold your head high. Be yourself and be proud of who you are. You're a beautiful, kind, loving person and if they show up, you'll have me, Robin and Jon by your side."

Charlie thrusts her chin in the air. "You're damn right. Let's go get our dates."

We head back arm-in-arm and as we do, I wonder how much my vanishing had to do with what Charlie said when it first started; she thought I wished it into being. It's true that not that long ago I wanted more than anything to disappear, to fade into the background.

How many times had I wished that before? How many years did it take to actually manifest and become real? Is there something in my DNA as Grandma Rose suggested that allowed it to happen? And if that's possible, then think of the potential I've unleashed. My real super power is in the discovery I can create with my thoughts.

From this moment on, I'm only letting the good in. I'm building my future one thought at a time.

Epilogue

My dreams of Gran are always the same. She's painting in her solarium when I walk into her apartment. I want desperately to hug and kiss her and tell her how much I love her, only I'm never allowed past the threshold. It's as if there's an invisible barrier keeping us apart.

She looks up, smiling and waving… and she always says the same thing. "I see you, Lola."

"What are you painting?" I call.

She tilts the canvas my way. It's a perfect rendering and I need no photograph to tell me who it is. It's me in my grad dress; hair and make-up perfect, looking like I do now, twenty pounds lighter.

Whenever I have this dream, I wake up immediately. I think it's because I'm supposed to remember it. And, of course, I do. I love that dream because it feels so real, like Gran and I are actually having a visit like we used to. Knowing that she sees me and knows what's happening in my life, gives me great comfort.

As I sit here now, in my room, I trace the rose on my wrist. That indelible gift from Gran, but more importantly, I feel the cord made of love connecting our hearts.

I live at home and commute to school. As hard as it would have been for me to believe a year ago, I now find comfort being with my family, especially Mom. Our relationship is growing as we're both changing. She's gone back to school, to the Revlon School of Beauty at my urging. And I've never seen her happier. I even let her practice on me, and that's something I never *ever* thought would happen.

Eva and I are also working on our relationship. At the very least, we're friends now. Things aren't perfect and there have been a few fights, but what's growing between us is a healthy respect. We even hang out occasionally.

University is a big change, but a positive one. My studies are going well. Of course, I'm an English major, but the best part is that so is Jon. We've grown even closer over the months and he's officially my boyfriend.

Charlie's still with Robin and works full time, but she's vowed that she will eventually go to college. She's holding down two jobs so that she can save enough for the tuition. We see each other a lot and even go on double dates.

As for Nino, he didn't come to the grad dance, after all. Tyler did, but kept his distance. Last I heard, Nino was working as a dump truck driver for his cousin's construction company. I know it's mean, but it gives me a little thrill thinking about him out there in the working world, his future already mapped out. Jon told me Nino had dreams of being a big-shot lawyer; probably only for the prestige and the money. But, like most bullies, he peaked in high school.

THE END

About the Author

Jeanne Bannon is a writer and freelance editor. She's worked in the publishing industry for over twenty years. Jeanne lives in Bolton, Ontario with her husband Dave and her two daughters, Nina and Sara. She's also the proud mother of two fur babies, Emily, a sweet Miniature Schnauzer and Spencer, a bratty Tabby with an attitude.

Acknowledgements

I want to thank my family for putting up with, and understanding, my obsessive need to write. Thanks to my husband, Dave, for never complaining and encouraging me to reach my dream. Thanks to my mother, Nina Bannon, for being my biggest champion and supporter and for reading and reviewing the early phases of the book. Thank you to my Aunt Catherine ("Kitty") Booth for believing in me. Thank you to Elena Cabral for your kindness and constant support. Jim Murini and Luigina Leonelli, I am grateful for your friendship and support.

Thank you to my publisher Solstice Publishing for liking my story enough to want to publish it and a special thank you to editors Candy Stone and Nik Morton for a job well done.

Last and certainly not least, thank you to my friends from the Next Big Writer. I could never have done this without you all. In particular Susan Stec, my BFF; Joy Campbell, my dear friend and mentor; Patti Yaeger, Alicia Perry; Wendy (WriteOn); JElizabeth and everyone else who took the time to read and review *Invisible* to help make it publishable.

Made in the USA
Charleston, SC
16 January 2014